Love is Forever Blue

DONALYN MAURER

Love is Forever Blue

Copyright © 2016 by Donalyn Maurer

Printed in the United States of America

First Printing, 2016

ISBN 0-9982510-1-1

Falling Anvil Publishing

123 Mesa Street

Scottsdale, AZ 00000

www.FallingAnvilBooks.com

TABLE OF CONTENTS

DEDICATION

To my children, my life.

Patrick, Regan and Julia

Some violence and sexual content. Recommended for mature audiences.

Three Months Earlier

After days in the hospital, it's good to be going home. My shoulder is still a little sore but the pain medication helps a lot. I have a small bandage covering the wound where Rocky shot me and I have to wear a sling for another week or two but the rest of me is feeling free and wonderful.

Sometimes guilt creeps in about the relief I feel knowing Rocky is dead, but I ignore it. It's like a weight has been lifted from my chest and I can finally breathe. The only thing is that he was the first person I ever gave myself to. I hold something in my heart for him because of that, and the knowledge of how damaged he was. The life full of pain he endured from his dad's abuse is something I know no one could survive without being affected.

Dr. Davis Jennings disappeared after everything happened at the cabin only to resurface a couple of days ago, not offering any explanation of his disappearance or his whereabouts. He came back to see his other son, Lincoln Jennings, who is doing better and is now out of ICU and in a private room. His mom, Lina, stays with him most days. Since Lina filed for divorce, she's refusing to go back to their house. Her friend, Lucy White, picked up some of her things for her.

Nick Callaghan, Linc's friend and neighbor who helps him out on his ranch, has stayed in town to help care for both Lina and Linc. As soon as Linc can travel, they're planning on heading back to their ranches in Lubbock.

Nick has also been down to check on my sister, Abigail, quite a few times. He's the one who grabbed her and took her to safety after Rocky stabbed her. He kept pressure on Abigail's wound and when Linc made it to them, although severely injured himself, he helped Nick stabilize her until the police and EMT's showed up. My family will be forever grateful to both Nick and Linc.

Max discussed moving in with me at my grandma's house with my dad and uncles. When I say discussed, I really think he told them there was no way in hell he was ever leaving my side ever again. I'm not sure of what exactly went down, but I'm told by Abigail and Violet that they heard yelling coming from my dad's home office where they were meeting. In the end, they agreed, although reluctantly, and gave their blessings to allow him to move in. My brothers and cousin didn't give him much of a hassle about it, which actually shocked me. I guess they know Max will take care of me and our grandma.

I'm beyond relieved. I want him with me. I don't think I can go back to being without him during our days and nights and I wouldn't want to.

When I fell for Maxwell "Blue" Bradshaw, I couldn't help but fall into him with everything I had in me.

CHAPTER ONE

By the time we arrive at the house, it's dinner time and all the family has gathered to once again welcome me home. When I step out of the car, the aroma from the smoker hits me and my stomach leaps for joy. Sausage and brisket. Oh, yeah.

Max helps me from the car and we make our way up the steps to the front door. My grandma, Aunt Savannah and Aunt Paige come around the corner from the kitchen and give me a hug, careful not to jostle my shoulder. A couple of seconds later, Abigail comes in on her crutches with Violet helping her. Abigail and I hug as best we can and then Violet takes me into her arms.

"Now, Jaycee I'm going to tell you what I told Abigail. If this is you girls' way of fishing for new jewelry, it worked this time." We all know she's trying to joke and ease the tension of almost losing both her daughters. She pulls out two velvet pouches and hands one to each of us. We both smile when we see JA on the pouch. It's a charm bracelet from James Avery. Each has a few charms, a cowboy boot, state of Texas, heart, cross, and one that says big sister on mine. Abigail's has the same except she has little sister on hers.

"Girls, from now on, how about you get your jewelry in the old fashioned traditional way, buy it, inherit it or have a man spoil you with it, but stop scaring me to death. When you scare me, I get emotional and when I get emotional about you girls, I get sentimental and then I go shopping. Shopping for jewelry apparently." She points at both of us. "You're going to get me in trouble with your daddy." At which time, Abigail and I both smile because we know if our big bad daddy is scared of anyone, it's Violet. "Although," she continues. "I should share that after your daddy started to gripe, I decided to show him what I was doing. The Texas charms, he picked. They're from him but I doubt he'll admit it." All three of us smile.

We walk into my grandma's kitchen and it looks fabulous since it was remodeled after the fire. Luckily, most of the damage was caused by smoke, not fire. It gave my dad a chance to update things for my grandma. It's an old house with just a simple kitchen, but my dad and uncles gave it nice facelift. She now has stainless steel appliances and granite counter tops. They replaced her old white cabinets with cherry wood, and added an island set up to double as a breakfast bar complete with stools lined up in front of it. The linoleum flooring has been replaced with hardwood flooring and it runs all the way into the dining room. My grandma told me he'd had people working around the clock. He'd tried to pay them but most insisted on doing the work on a volunteer basis.

Set up on the kitchen island is the normal essentials we always have when we barbecue. Beans, potato salad, coleslaw, chips and our homemade barbecue sauce. Someone has made one of my sister's favorites, fruit salad and one of my favorites, carrot salad with raisins and powdered sugar.

Before I can start picking at the food, Max pulls me into my bedroom and closes the door. I jolt to a stop and slowly look around to take it all in. There's so much I can't believe it. It's beautiful. My old bed with wood frame has been replaced with a beautiful wrought iron four-poster canopy frame with white lace valances hanging down. The headboard is stunning in its design. It reminds me of a live oak tree with branches are growing wild in every direction. The bed covers are a brilliant white with lace trimming and there are half a dozen throw pillows in different shades of pink. I immediately know my Aunt Paige had her hand in this. Looking at the windows, I see old style lace draped over the rod and hanging all the way to the floor. And my carpet is gone. It's been replaced with a throw rug over the same hardwood floor that was in the kitchen and dining room. From the ceiling, an antique looking miniature chandelier hangs. The dresser, night stands and chester drawer are all oversized ivory and look worn. At the foot of the bed, there's an old cushioned bench with big brass tacks and a patchwork quilt with different pastel colors hangs across it. A few prints of wildflowers are on one wall and then another wall full of old family photos. I make my way to them and my eyes slowly travel across them. I can tell this is my Aunt Savannah's work.

Frames of all shapes and sizes hang with various pictures of our family over the years. Pictures at the lake, our cabin, Easter and Halloween get-togethers, Christmas pictures of us with Santa and opening presents around the Christmas tree. There's one of me around two years old, standing in my grandpa's old cowboy boots with an empty beer bottle to my lips. I laugh thinking how not much about me has changed. When my eyes hit one picture in particular, my breath leaves me. My eyes water but I rub the moisture away so I can focus on the picture. Stepping closer, I touch the frame and a smile touches my lips. The old worn picture is in a beautiful brass frame and it's of me and my grandpa. He's standing in our cabin holding me on his hip. I'm looking up at him laughing and he's smiling down at me. I have to be about five years old and I'm barefoot, wearing a little blue sundress with sunflowers on it. In the background, all over the counters in the kitchen and on the table, coffee cans with blue bonnets are scattered. I remember that dress and I remember that day. I'd been sad because my grandpa had been out on the lake all day with my brothers while I stayed at the cabin with my grandma. It was the day before the rest of the family came up for a couple of days. Grandma and I spent the day getting extra linens ready and airing out cots and roll out beds. This was the day we'd have fifteen or more people sleeping in the same room. The same room as the breakfast area and kitchen. We'd cook out, go skiing, swim at the beach, play games in the field, hunt for snipes in the woods and head down to the lake with our lawn chairs to catch the sunset by the dock. The lake's dam sat not too far away and at night it was lit with beautiful blue lights. My grandpa would take my grandma out for a sunset ride in the boat and they always took me; those memories are the ones I cherish the most. Grandpa would make me wear an old giant orange life jacket that doubled as a pillow. I'd lie down between their seats in the boat and fall asleep to the feel of the boat crashing gently over the waves and then I'd fake sleep so my grandpa would carry me from the boat. For the rest of the night, he'd held me up against his chest and shoulder while I slept. He sat back in his lawn chair on the dock, with me, and visited with the rest of the family. My heart swells remembering how he told me how glad he was to get back to his pretty girl, giving me kisses all over my face to make me laugh. I smile at the memory with happy tears in my eyes.

"If I had only one wish, ever in my life, it would be that you could have known him. He'd love you as much as I do." I whisper to Max. He wraps his arms around my waist and holds me.

"Me too. I remember seeing him with your brothers at school events; I met him a couple of times." he says softly against my ear.

Feeling my breathing start to hiccup, I take a deep breath and move away to continue looking around. I notice a couple pictures on the nightstand and walk over to them. My sister must have taken them. One is of Max sitting on a chair in my hospital room. He's looking out the window in thought as he absently plays his guitar. He looks handsome and deep in his own thoughts. The other one is of Max and I asleep in the hospital bed. He's laying on his side, facing me and my head is cradled into his shoulder and chest; our arms around each other's waist. His head is resting on the top of mine. I turn to find him watching me with tenderness in his eyes.

7

I walk over to him and drop my forehead on his chest as he wraps his arms around me. "Max, I don't know why God sent you to me, but I'm so thankful," I whisper. His arms pull me tighter to him.

"Me too, Jayc." he says as he lowers his lips to my ear. They travel to my cheek where he kisses me. He just stays there, his lips to my skin. I turn into them and rest my lips to his. I don't kiss him and he doesn't kiss me for a few moments, each of us allowing our warm breaths to mingle. Finally, he adds pressure as he separates his lips and he runs his tongue along the seam of my lips. I open for him and we taste each other slowly, savoring. We kiss softly, taking our time; each content that we can do this now. After a few minutes, there's a knock on the door. Max steps back with a soft smile and leaves my side to open the door. My Aunt Savannah and Paige, Violet, Grandma and Abigail step in the room one by one; the amazing women who did this all for me. I take steadying breaths, trying to control my emotions and the deep sense of gratitude for what they did for me. Max walks back to me and gives me a kiss on the cheek, telling me he's going outside with the men. He's had enough emotional stuff to last a lifetime, he informs us, which breaks the tension and we start to laugh.

After he leaves, the girls show me the rest of the work they did. Violet explains my dad wanted me to have fresh memories. I finally notice new clothes in the closet, and a beautiful ivory pedestal sink in the bathroom replacing the old wood vanity. The shower is now tiled in a chocolate colored stone with built in shelves and glass door. All the fixtures are gold worn brass and the towels are mint green and peach. Little knickknacks line one of the shelves and an old freestanding cross with two cowboys on their horses is carved into the wood. The window is now double paned with a security lock and they've installed an old crank handle with wooden shutters. It compliments the bathroom perfectly. Just outside the bathroom is a full size antique looking mirror on a stand. It's absolutely breathtaking. All of it. The women tell me how the men gave them part of the insurance money and told them to "do it up." I also note there are newly installed smoke alarms in the bathroom and bedroom along with an alarm panel. I hadn't noticed but I guess they've installed a home alarm. Violet tells me all the windows and doors are hooked up to the alarm and if anyone tries to enter, after it's been set, the alarm will sound and send a distress call to the police. Same for the doors. As we start to leave my bedroom to join the men, I pause. On the dresser, there's an old pair of cowboy boots decorated with flowers and used for vases. And laying in front of them is a long slender case wrapped in a velvet pouch. I open it to find Violet has replaced the pearls she'd given me that were damaged in the fire. I run my fingers along them before meeting her eyes.

"Violet, thank you. But you didn't have to do this," I take a deep breath and release it while still staring at the pearls.

"Yes. Yes, I did. I absolutely did. Insurance covered the cost but I wanted to replace them. Not have you do it. I wanted them to come from my hands to yours." We both smile and I hug her as I lay them back in their case before we walk out to join our men.

CHAPTER TWO

Outside, my dad and uncles are sitting in lawn chairs, talking and having a few beers. The smoker is a few feet away filling the air with the delicious scent of cooked meat. Jake must have set up the dartboard because they have a game going a few feet away from a table scattered with beer bottles and flight tips.

My dad stands to give me a hug and kiss before helping Abigail to the table. Uncle Duke is checking the smoker and after he closes it, he joins us. He has his arm around Aunt Savannah and me and when I hear a collective yell, I smile and look over at the guys playing darts. They're all joking around caught up in their game. I start to make my way to Max but stop when Uncle Brock speaks up.

"Hey, everyone? Paige and I have an announcement." We turn towards them and the guys come over from the dartboard. Max pulls me to him and wraps his arm around my waist. "We have something we want to share." Aunt Paige looks down, but not before I see sadness fill her eyes.

I'm getting scared and I look around and I can see I'm not the only one. What he says next, sends everyone's heart breaking it two.

"As some of you know the adoption agency called us a couple of months ago letting us know we had a baby, a son. Although we were disappointed, we were also happy when the mother decided to keep her baby. She was a teenager and was scared to tell her parents about the pregnancy. When she finally did, they stepped up to help her. She never really wanted to give him up. We prayed long and hard and we know in the end, it was the right thing for the baby. A little over a week ago, we received another call about a baby that had been abandoned in the hospital. He was sick. No one knew how sick, though. Most of the foster parents declined to step up. With their plates already being full fostering others I think they were worried it would be touch much, I guess. When our social worker heard of the situation, they called us and asked for our help," Uncle Brock tells us.

"We went to visit him, Cole, we named him Cole," he adds, running a hand down his face. "At the hospital and he was extremely sick." He coughs and clears his throat from emotion as my Aunt Paige turns into his chest and starts to sniffle. "His birth mom, she was sick, too. There were rumors she used drugs while she was pregnant with Cole but we don't know for sure." He takes a deep breath and pulls my aunt Paige even closer to him.

"We were able to spend a few days with him while he fought but finally God saw fit to end his pain and struggle. The Lord called him home three days ago, early morning. His birth mom, she walked out of the hospital the morning she delivered him without saying a word or signing any papers and no one has heard from her, or any of her family. The father is unknown. The state was going to give Cole a pauper burial..." Gasps of anger are heard from my family and Uncle Brock puts his hand out to calm everyone. "It's just the way it's done. No one liked the idea. Not the social workers. Not the nurses or doctors and not Paige and I. We talked to the social worker and the adoption agency and even though Cole passed before any paperwork was signed, the court decided to allow us to become his legal guardians. Cole Jaxson McGinty, was, is, our son. We wanted him to have a name and a family." He looks at all of us. "That's us." We all nod in agreement. "Tomorrow, we'll lay him to rest in a small ceremony and we'd like you all to be there for him." There's not one of us that would deny such a request.

"We received more news after Cole's passing. Our social worker came to the hospital the day he passed and told us Cole has a big sister, Callie. She's a little over three years old and even before Cole's birth, her mom had been in and out of her life. She's been in the care of her great aunt but she's elderly and taken ill. She can't take care of her anymore so she's asked the state to come get her. With her mom nowhere to be found and because of her abandoning Cole, the state has moved to terminate all her parental rights but this process will take some time. They're going to allow her to be adopted after some legal issues are cleared up. The social worker set us up to meet and visit with Callie, and after those visits, Paige and I decided we're going to be Callie's foster parents. When she's completely free, we're going to petition to adopt her."

Aunt Paige finally speaks. "She's absolutely beautiful. Long blonde hair with ringlets all around and the biggest eyes that are almost silver. When she smiles, her

dimples pop out and her little button nose crinkles up."
Aunt Paige gushes with love. "The time we've spent with
her, the few visits, we're in love and she's taken to us." She
looks at her husband and smiles with love and admiration.
"She's already in love with him it seems." She looks back at
us. "The day after tomorrow, we're picking her up and
bringing her home with us." Her face lights up into a smile
so bright it could warm the sun. "Tomorrow, if you ladies
are up to it, I need help. So much to prepare for her. She
needs everything, clothes and furniture. I mean I have to
get the right shampoos, baby food...wait, she won't eat baby
food? A high chair or booster? A bed, childproof the house,
car seats..." She falls silent. "Brock, oh my, how are we
going to do all that? We'll never have it all ready for her.
And sweet Cole...we have to...."

I can see it all beginning to overwhelm her
emotionally and my grandma must see it too. She steps
forward and pulls her into a hug,

"Oh, honey, I am so sorry for your heartbreak; but
I'm happy for y'all and little Callie. We'll have everything
ready for her when she finally comes home. We'll divide up
chores after Cole's service. Some of the men can get her
furniture and put it together while the others childproof
the house and install car seats and such." She looks at the
men who are all quiet but enthusiastically nodding their
heads. "And us," she points to the women, "we'll handle the
bows, ribbons, ruffles and lace." We all give her soft smiles.
"We'll go to the grocery store and stock up on anything and
everything, okay?" Aunt Paige smiles at her with gratitude
and love and Uncle Brock looks at his mom, my grandma

with so much love it even fills my heart. "Thanks, Mom." He says and steps from Aunt Paige to embrace her.

"You two..." she looks between them, "ya'll deserve this so much. I'm so sorry about little Cole. We'll be there to support you with him and then help you get things ready for Callie." She pats him on the arm and then steps back as the rest of the family steps forward with mixed emotion over the loss of a precious child but also wanting to celebrate in the saving of another.

While the men pull the brisket and sausage from the smoker, the women go inside and get the plates, napkins, cups and silverware and a pitcher of sweet tea. We bring it outside along with all the side foods. Uncle Duke is slicing the meat while my brothers pull a couple of saw horses from the garage along with big piece of wood left over from the remodeling and set up makeshift table big enough to seat all of us. We pull our mismatched chairs up to the table and once everyone is settled, we join hands and say grace. We give thanks for so many things. I'm giving thanks for Max and my family. A prayer is sent up for Cole, Rocky and the Jennings' family. I smile as I think of Callie. She's coming to the right family. A precious little girl with all these protective men. She'll be so loved. Just like Abigail and I.

Later that night, after everyone has gone home and grandma has gone to bed, I sit swinging on the porch swing staring up at the stars, while Max picks up the last of the beer bottles. After he throws them in the recycling bin he grabs his car keys from our room and walks to his car to grab his bags from the trunk.

It's a beautiful night and there's not a cloud in the sky. The porch light is off and with no city lights or street lamps around, the stars are shining brilliantly overhead. It takes me back to summer nights at the lake. Tonight, this night sky, it rivals those. Maybe it's just being alive and free that's making the stars seem to shine brighter or food to taste better, love to feel deeper and stronger, but whatever it is, it's making me appreciate and not take things for granted.

"Hey, Jayc?" Max sits his bags down by the screen door and walks over and sits next to me. "You okay?"

I smile at him, but then I have a flashback. Pain from the past hits out of nowhere and I can't help but frown when I think about what I've put my family through and what I've put him through. He sees this and frowns so I look down to my lap. No matter how good I'm feeling, guilt and fear creeps in. The therapist had warned me this might happen. Fear stepping back in; it's normal but I can't help feeling overwhelmed. Doubt rushes forward in my thoughts and I become unsure of everything. I need to give him an out even though it would kill me if he walks away. The thought of him not being by my side brings a wave of pain across me so deep it knocks the breath from me. No matter what, I'm damaged now and it's going to take time to heal. Max may not have counted on all this extra baggage from the past and the long process healing moving forward is going to be.

"Max, if you would have known you were going to

have to go through all of this danger and pain, would you have stayed away or have you thought of going away now? I mean, if you stayed with me because I was hurt, I'll be okay now so I'd understand if you need or want to walk away. I won't blame you if you do." I say quietly. "I just want you to be happy," I whisper to my hands.

I sit, praying he won't take the out I'm offering. He cups my face and pulls it up so he can look into my eyes. He stares at me for a few moments, not speaking, and it's making me nervous. Finally, he leans in and kisses me. I can't help but sigh in relief. He's not showing me with his words. He's giving his answer through his kiss. We kiss for a few minutes before he pulls back. What he says next calms my doubts and warms my heart.

"Jaycee, if I would have known you were going to be in danger, would I have stayed away? If you were in pain or hurt, would I leave you because you're better or not?" His eyes search my face as he frowns as he thinks about my words and then looks a little angry. "Is that what you're really asking me?" I nod and pull my face from his hands and bow my head but he puts his finger to my chin and lifts my face back to him making me look in his eyes. "My love, if I would have known that you were going to go through all this," he leans into and whispers in my ear, "I would have run as fast as I could to you. To protect you. Never away from you, Jaycee. I would have jumped in front of you and taken it all so you would never have to feel pain. I would gladly done that for you," he says, his warm breath sends chills across my body.

I crawl into his lap and kiss him. After a moment of heavy kissing, my lips travel down the side of his face to his neck. I stop there and bury my face, breathing in his scent, letting the calm it brings me wash over me. We stay like this, wrapped up together, for a while as he swings us. When a chill starts to hit the air, he cradles me as he stands and then puts me on my feet. "Come on." he says and takes my hand, opening the door and leading me in. He grabs his bags with one hand, keeping mine in his other and we start for my, our, bedroom. Once inside, he puts his stuff on the bench at the end of the bed and I excuse myself as I go into the bathroom. Using my good arm, I brush my teeth, face and my hair. When I walk out, the only thing Max is wearing is his jeans. They're unbuttoned and hanging loose and I can see his light patch of hair on his chest running down across his abs and into his boxers. I stand and stare, following the trail, like a creep. "You done?" he asks. I blush red, embarrassed, but nod yes because I'm not sure if he's asking about me staring or asking about the bathroom. Plus, speaking right now is impossible. He sends me a knowing smile before walking into the bathroom.

"Damn, that man is fine," I whisper to myself as I start looking through my drawers for pajamas I'm certain Aunt Paige would have bought. After searching most of the drawers, I only find a few silky gowns trimmed in lace. *Alrighty then.* I raise the sling off my arm and unbutton my shirt and pull it off, letting it fall to the floor along with my bra. I can move my shoulder fairly good even though it's still sore. I just can't raise it too high or carry anything yet.

I push my jeans down my legs and kick them off before picking up the gown that's royal blue with black lace. It's pretty short so I'll be surprised if reaches past my upper thighs or covers my butt, I realize with a shake of my head. Since I can't lift my shoulder, I step into the gown then shimmy it up, slipping the straps over my shoulders before smoothing it down my body enjoying the feel of the silk. Okay, good. I breathe out a sigh. So much easier that way. I start to turn when I feel Max's hands grip my hips tight as he pulls me back against him.

"Damn, Jaycee, watching you move like that, pulling your nightie up over your legs, hips and tits was fucking sexy." He reaches down to where the lace falls against the very tops of my thighs and traces it with his fingers. "Jayc, I know you're hurt, so tell me to stop," he whispers into my neck.

Is he crazy? I relax into him and drop my head back on his shoulder, closing my eyes to enjoy the feeling of his touch. His fingers start to pull the hem of the gown up.

"Tell me to stop." he whispers again. *Yup. He's crazy*.

Not going to happen. I push back against him and then lift my hands and rub them up my tummy and across the silk to my breasts. I know he likes when I touch myself so it surprises me when he reaches around and grabs my wrists to stop me. He turns and walks us across the room and stops in front of full length mirror. He pulls my wrists down to my side and I watch him as he looks up my body slowly, finally meeting my eyes with his. He reaches down

19

and intertwines our fingers and wraps his arms around me, holding me tight for a few moments while resting his face in my neck. I watch as he turns his face into my neck and trails light kisses on my neck. He releases our fingers and flattens my hands beneath his on my hips and begins moving them down to where the lace is resting against my thighs.

"Now, touch yourself," he says and starts lifting my gown with my own hands beneath his.

When we get past my panties, he releases his hold on mine and has me grip the gown in place. He uses one of his hands to gather my hair and pull my head back and to the side as he starts kissing down my neck. His other hand travels down my tummy, into my panties and his finger starts circling. I moan and turn my head to give him better access to my neck but he stops.

"Jaycee, look at me," he demands. I meet his eyes in the mirror. "Am I hurting you?"

I shake my head and beg. "No, Max. Please, keep going. Don't stop..." before all the words are out of my mouth, he goes back to kissing and running his warm tongue along my neck as his hand and fingers go back to rubbing me.

He circles and then pushes inside me a little and he keeps doing this until I feel like I'm going to scream. I try moving my hips but he's holding me still by my hair and every time I shift, he tightens his grip sending me a message to keep still. I'm so close to losing it and turning around and attacking him.

"Love, touch yourself, your tits." I don't even think twice, I just obey. "Lower the straps off your shoulders, slowly," and I do it, one side at a time and then look back to him for approval. "Give me your fingers." He opens his mouth and I lift two of my fingers to him. He brings his mouth down and I watch him in the reflection as he wets them with light sucks and licks. My entire body spasms at the feel of his mouth on my fingers. When he pulls his head back, he catches my eyes.

"Rub your nipples with those fingers," he instructs me and with him our hands intertwined, I reach down and touch myself, lightly pinching my nipple; moaning at how good it feels. I keep doing it as he starts using two fingers on me. He releases my hair and brings his hand down against my tummy, holding me against him while his other is moving in and out of me; circling my most sensitive area.

"Pinch your nipples harder," he demands. The second I do as he says, he slides his hand down my hip and into my panties from behind, entering me. The sensation of both his hands working my body over is starting to drive me crazy.

"Come on, Jaycee. Let me see." He bites my neck, and that's all it takes. I let go and scream as he brings his mouth down on mine; capturing my cries. His hands continue to move, helping me to ride out my orgasm. My scream and moans are his. They belong to him and he consumes them with his kiss. His arms tighten around me, keeping me from falling to the ground in a puddle. Once I come down, he holds me for a few moments before he loosens his arms and gently pulls his hands from me; stepping back. I'm barely aware of my gown sliding from my body and falling to the ground. He steps forward, puts his fingers in the sides of my panties, and pulls them slowly down my legs. He steers me to the bed, guiding me onto the pillows. Even in my daze, the soft, cool sheets feel good.

Max takes his jeans and boxers off and begins to stroke himself. My body spasms and comes back to life as I watch him. *Holy heck!* I can't control the moan that escapes me at the hot sight of him stroking himself. He climbs on the bed and lays next to me, covering my mouth with his. His hand travels back down to me, and the minute he touches me, I know he can feel I'm more than ready. I reach for him, to pull him on top of me as I whisper my plea to him in the quiet of the room.

"Please, Max. Please. Now." I want him inside me. I need him. I yank him closer and open for him at the same time. He comes willingly and softly brings himself down on top of me. He leans down and kisses my neck, licking up behind my ear. Shivering, I scratch my nails down his back and he shudders and groans. His hands glide up my back between the mattress and my body. When he reaches the back of my head, he grips my hair and pulls my neck back. It's harsh and gentle at same time, and I can tell he's taking care to be cautious of my shoulder.

"I love your long hair, Jaycee, fucking love it," he whispers in my ear as he gives it another gentle but strong tug. I feel my breathing quicken and I open myself more; trying to lift my hips to meet his. He pulls his head back and brings his eyes down to look at me. As he starts to enter me, my lips part and my eyes start to close.

"Jayc. No. Look at me," he says. I look back at him as he pushes the rest of the way inside. I stare but my mouth drops open in a moan as his bottom lips drops and his eyes go hooded. He doesn't release my hair or my eyes as he starts moving.

"Jesus, Jayc, you feel so good." He lowers his head to my breasts and starts gently sucking them and licking them. My hips move to meet his as I bring my hand up to hold him in place and let my other travel down his back feathering my nails along his beautiful olive skin. He bucks and picks up his speed as he starts going deeper.

"Jaycee, I'm almost there, hurry." I pull his head further into me.

"Please, Max." I plead. He understands I need more and sucks hard on my nipple and gently bites at the same time. That does it and I explode again, releasing a quiet moan as I call his name. Once I settle, he raises a little and starts thrusting faster.

"Beautiful, Jayc." He releases my hair, pulls his arms back and collapses on his elbows, bringing his hands to hold the side of my face as his thumbs gently stroke my cheeks, still keeping eye contact. He starts pushing into me harder so I lift my knees to his sides, allowing him to go even deeper. His eyes turn glassy and at the same time I feel a tear slide out of my eye and into my hair. We're both realizing we could have lost this, lost each other. No words are needed to express the love we're feeling at this moment. One of my hands is on his back with my nails digging in gently and the other is wrapped around his waist where I'm pulling him forward. When he gets there, he buries his face in my neck and lets out a long groan as he finds his release. After a few minutes, he lifts his head and we both smile sleepily at each other. He leans down and kisses me, a beautiful soft, kiss that I don't want to end, disappointed when he pulls back first.

He gets up and walks into the bathroom, coming back with a warm washcloth to clean me. After, he leans down and gives me another kiss and pulls the covers over me. He walks back to the bathroom door and tosses the washcloth in the hamper. As he's coming back to the bed, he stops and picks something up off the floor before returning to my side.

"Sit up, Jayc." I do as he says and he lowers the sling over my shoulder, positioning my arm in it. "Love, did I hurt you?" I look up and smile.

"No. Not at all, Max." When he finally gets back in bed, he pulls the sheets over himself and reaches for me. I go to him and lay my head on his chest with my injured shoulder resting easily across his chest.

"I love you, Max." I whisper.

He brings his arm up and pulls me closer. "Love you too, Jayc. Forever and a day. Because forever will never be long enough." We both fall asleep within minutes wrapped in the comfort of his words.

CHAPTER THREE

We rise early the next morning. We have to make the one-hour drive to Kerr County to lay baby Cole to rest. Uncle Brock and Aunt Paige received word that even after Cole's passing, the judge granted the adoption with special circumstances and allowed the name to go on the birth certificate with them listed as his parents. They made phone calls to Lex, our second cousin, at the funeral home and to Mama Boudouin, Aunt Paige's mom. Mama Boudouin got on the phone with their pastor from Church of Christ and arranged for a small service to be held this morning. Following the service, we'll take him to the Boudouin family cemetery that lies on a hill at the back of their property. Lex promised them he'd take care of the rest. He'd get Cole from the hospital, then to the church and to the cemetery. He refused payment of any kind, telling them they were family. I think we all feel bad about being scared of him. It seems he shares the same heart of gold as his cousin, my grandpa.

My grandma is riding with Max and I to the church. During the drive, she tells us that the social worker who spoke to the judge about Cole, told Aunt Paige and Uncle Brock that as she explained to the judge, my aunt and uncle still wanted to follow through with the adoption, even though Cole passed. The judge had signed the papers with teary eyes, touched not only for the loss of Cole, but the beautiful gift my aunt and uncle were giving him. We all feel that way.

We arrive at the church at almost the same time as the rest of the family. Pulling into the large gravel church parking lot, we see it's full except for a few open spots, side by side. Heading into the church sanctuary, I wonder if there's a service that will be letting out before Cole's begins. A man who looks about the same age as my dad approaches us. He's in blue jeans, a white snap down western shirt, boots and a tan stetson.

"Mornin', I'm Jace Mays, the pastor. Ya'll must be Brock and Paige's family." My dad steps forward and shakes his hand. "Yes, we're the McGinty's. Good to meet you; just wish it were under better circumstances."

Pastor Mays looks down and shakes his head. "It's a shame. Such a young precious life, gone too soon. After Paige's momma called and told my wife and I what happened, my wife got on the phone and started making calls. She believes that little baby deserves a big send off. Seems our entire congregation," he glances around the parking lot and back to the church, "has shown up along with most of the town sharing that feeling. Some folks' carpooled in knowing the lot would fill up. They left those spots for y'all." He gestures to the spots we just parked in. "Y'all can go on inside. We'll be starting in a few minutes. I just came out to collect my thoughts. I got a little overwhelmed when I walked in and saw the sanctuary. Y'all may want to prepare yourselves." With that, he nods and heads back inside.

When we enter the sanctuary's vestibule, we stop and stare, shocked and overwhelmed just like Pastor Mays warned us we would be. Tears fall from my eyes as my grandma and Aunt Savannah pull tissues from their purses and start handing them out. I take one and wipe my eyes as Max pulls me to him. Collective coughs and throat clearing come from the men standing with us as we all face the church's altar.

The tiniest, shiny, silver and blue coffin sits at the alter. On top, lies a cross made from blue and white flowers. Although sadly beautiful, what catches my heart is what has been placed around it.

Toys are spread all around Cole's little coffin; a firetruck and some matchbox cars, blocks and a little blue tricycle. As we walk closer, I notice baby rattles and stuffed animals, toy soldiers and a wooden rocking horse. There's even a red wagon with a giant stuffed elephant sitting in it. The sight of all the things that should have been Cole's is enough to have my heart breaking in two.

The pews are packed with people and its standing room only. Blue balloons are all around the church. I stand in awe of this until I see my Uncle Brock and Aunt Paige start walking towards us. Neither speak, they just gesture for us to sit up front with them and Aunt Paige's family. Shortly after we take our seats, Aunt Paige's family members and ours exchange quiet hello's. Moments later, Pastor Mays comes in.

Everyone sits in silence as he recites an opening

prayer. He goes on offering no reasons or justifications for the loss of this little life. He explains that these are the times he has to let go of trying to make sense and turn it all over to God. He recites the poem, "Footprints in the Sand" to assure us, Cole, in his short journey here with us, was never ever alone and that he's sure God himself comes to bring the children home.

The congregation stands to say the benediction and then we make our way back out to our cars. As we walk, I find myself still wiping my eyes and taking deep breaths trying to relieve some of the tightness in my chest from my heart breaking for little Cole. I'm not the only one affected; men hold their women while wiping their tears, talk softly and give one arm hugs. Parents walk with their children, pulling them closer as they realize how blessed they are to have them here. As we reach our car and open the doors to sit down, my grandma leans over and takes my hand and holds it tight for a few moments before letting go.

We line up for the short drive to the Boudouin's family cemetery with the hearse leading the way. We park in a field that runs beside an old iron fence that surrounds the graves. The hearse pulls inside the gates and up alongside a newly dug grave. As Max holds me close, my chest becomes tight again as tears fall. Cole is gently and lovingly placed above the grave on a grate by Lex and others from the funeral home. My heart and mind are torn between the beautiful care and heartache of the reality of watching a child placed to his final rest. The people from the church and town pull up the hill and exit their cars, crowding into the small cemetery with many having to stand outside the fence. They, just like me are touched. Many hold hands and link arms. I briefly wonder if they know each other or if they are strangers so deeply touched they find the need to reach out to one another for support. They're holding the balloons from the church and some of the toys. After Pastor Mays says a short opening prayer, Jesse steps forward with his guitar and pulls the strap over his shoulder. He starts strumming and everyone falls silent. Jesse rarely plays and sings for anyone. It's his private gift. When he starts singing, everyone goes quiet and listens, surprised by the soft beauty of his voice. When the chorus starts, the crowd starts to softly sing along with him between their tears as they tell baby Cole to go rest high on that mountain. After the song finishes, Pastor Mays gives the final prayer and we release the balloons. Over a hundred blue balloons rise into the air, heading for Heaven as the children in the crowd start clapping and laughing which makes everyone smile and take shuttering breaths. I stand and stare at the sky watching as the blue balloons disappear. Rest in peace, Cole Jaxson McGinty.

A long line of cars and trucks travel down the old dirt road that leads to the family's farmhouse. It's a beautiful plantation style house nestled in between the trees. The house is bright white with red shutters and a wide, covered porch. Chairs and rockers line one side and a porch swing hangs on the other side with more chairs. There are even ceiling fans spinning slowly that help keep you cool while sitting outside in the Texas heat. I visited here a few times when Aunt Paige's grandparents still lived there. After both her grandparents passed, her mom and dad moved here from the city and took over running the estate. I've been in love with the house and land since my first visit. Behind the house, there's a dirt road that leads to an old red barn that's not used anymore. A newer barn is down a road not far from the house. The cars pull up and people start climbing out, carrying food covered with foil and bags. As they head towards the house, a couple of women standing on the front porch start taking the bags and setting them aside before they continue on into the house with their covered dishes. My dad and Violet lead the way as we walk up to the porch. A very pretty brunette with beautiful blue eyes smiles down at us in greeting.

"Hi, I'm Bobbie Sue Mays."

"Pastor Mays' wife?" Violet asks.

"Yes, Pastor Mays' wife." She points to the bags, "I'm going to start taking these down to the storage area in the new barn. It's donations for Callie. I tell you, small towns, the love they show is incredible. I grew up in a bigger town and although we were close, it wasn't like this." She starts picking up bags when Jake, Jesse, Nash, Chase, Connor, Bradley and Max step up and grab them from her.

"Okay. Well, thank you," she smiles at their gesture and they follow her to the barn. Uncle Brock comes out and shakes hands with his brothers and hugs the women. I look around and see I'm not the only one touched by this outpouring. Others are taking it all in as well. One woman, with the most beautiful blonde hair stands silently off to the side quietly crying and, taking everything in, like me. A man towing the cutest red tricycle with a basket and horn with ribbons falling from the handle bars notices her crying quietly too. He goes to her and they speak softly to each before she pulls him into an embrace before standing back and looking at all the gifts being given for Callie. He and I both watch as she gives a tight smile, turns and starts back towards the cars parked out front. I take a deep breath; my throat and chest tight from all the emotion being shown by everyone.

We stay, have brunch and talk with many wonderful people. The beauty of the countryside and the kindness of the people here draws me in; I can imagine moving and living here forever. Before Max and I leave, we decide to walk down to the barn to grab a few bags to take back to town so we can lighten the load for my aunt and uncle. When we reach the barn, we stop and look around. Again, this community proves to be amazing. The outpouring of love they've shown, not only for Cole but for Callie is beyond measure. Someone has gone through the bags and sorted things between clothes, toys, food not only for Callie but for Uncle Brock and Aunt Paige. There's bedding and wall decorations fitting for a little girl. A few dolls are along the wall with over a dozen pair of shoes ranging from dress shoes to sneakers to sandals and a couple of pairs of little girl cowboy boots. There's a pink cowboy hat, dresses, overalls, blue jeans and tops, and a bunch of beautiful little girl gowns and also footed pajamas. The red tricycle sits across the room along with a dollhouse and red wagon. A piece of paper with a picture catches my eye and I walk forward to see what it is. It's a receipt marked 'paid' with a picture of wooden jungle gym. It has a tire swing off one end and a twisty slide off the other. Max and I turn towards each other and he shakes his head, both of us amazed at the volume of things donated.

Aunt Paige arrives and gasps, her hands flying up to cover her mouth. Aunt Paige barely had time to recover when Uncle Brock entered the barn, his step faltering as he approached his wife. Several emotions played across his features as he drew Aunt Paige to his side, his voice thick when he finally spoke. "Um, yeah. I think we're going to need a bigger truck."

"Yep, A really big truck." Max replies.

"They've thought of everything, Brock. Look. Everything." He nods.

"Well, I guess y'all go on and take off. I'm going to go talk to Stone and Duke and your brothers about loading this up." He leans down and gives Aunt Paige a kiss before taking one last look around, shaking his head. We share a smile with Aunt Paige; it seems as though little baby Cole took care of his mom, dad and sister from Heaven.

Max and I head back into town but we make a quick stop at home to change. Max is going to do some painting and putting up decorations; I'll be stuck watching him because of my shoulder. When we walk into our bedroom, I stand still and take in the beauty of the room and all the thought and love put into it. Max comes up behind me and wraps me in his arms resting his chin on my head.

"I don't think I've ever seen anything like today and

I don't think I ever will again, Jayc." I nod and turn around in his arms to look at him.

"I know. I mean, there are no words." I slide my hand up his chest and wrap it behind his neck. "Max, today I went through every emotion I've ever had." He nods in agreement before we silently change our clothes and head over to get things ready for Callie's arrival.

CHAPTER FOUR

When we pull up to Uncle Brock and Aunt Paige's two story white stone home, we see about half the family is already there. The men. It figures. Today was emotional and although I know they felt it, enough was probably enough. We walk up the sidewalk right as Jesse opens the door to run out to his truck and get something.

"Hey Brat, Blue," he says and starts to walk off but I reach out and grab his arm, stopping him. I pull him into a hug surprising him. After a moment he softens and gives a tight hug back before releasing me and quickly walking off. I'm so proud of what he did for Cole today.

Walking through the threshold of the house with Max, I study the cherry wood door that is mostly frosted glass. The scripted *M* in the center that stands for McGinty is a signature piece that I've always loved. It looks so serene against their white stone house. They have a couple of old wooden benches on their front porch and rows of potted plants. In the front yard, off to the side, stands a Magnolia tree but there's no blooms now. I love that tree. One day, I want one of my own. I think every southern girl should have her very own Magnolia tree.

Their house has an open floor plan downstairs. The kitchen is in the center and it's one of the most awesome kitchens I've ever seen. The countertops are tiled red along with the backsplash with a few random white ones thrown in here and there. Their appliances are all stainless steel and her cabinets are a deep cherry wood like the front door. On the counter sits an old cowboy boot being used as a vase and it's holding sunflowers just like the ones sitting on my dresser in my bedroom.

We hear voices and head up the winding wood staircase to the landing. There's a large bay window with a seating area built in with a cushion and throw pillows. Off to the side, there's a chaise that's a dark cream color, an odd-shaped coffee table with only three legs and an inviting sofa and loveseat with baby blue and white stripes. The walls are decorated with random shelves holding books or small vases with flowers and black and white pictures of them, dating back from their high school days to the present.

Off to the right of that room, is the guest room. It's has a warm, old-fashioned feel with simple furniture and a beautiful quilt laying across the bed. Walking past that, we finally reach what is now Callie's room. It's been taped up and the floor is covered. Uncle Duke is kneeling next to a paint can, mixing and complaining, trying to convince Bradley to do the painting. Uncle Duke looks up and sees us and smiles.

"Thank God." He stands and hands Max the roller and paint pan. "I hate painting and Bradley here," he gestures with his thumb over his shoulder at Bradley, "won't help his old dad out." Bradley rolls his eyes behind his dad's back. "I can tape and float all day but just can't do the painting," Uncle Duke says and walks away leaving us standing in the middle of the room looking at his back.

Max turns to me and Bradley. "I think he hates painting."

"You think, sugar bear?" I ask with a laugh.

He grins at my pet name and his dimples show in all their glory.

Bradley laughs as he leaves the room following his dad. "Sugar bear."

He continues laughing as he walks down the stairs. Max looks at me in question, expectantly waiting an explanation.

"Yes, sugar bear." I nod with all seriousness and explain. "Well, you started calling me love, and I swoon every time you do."

He drops the roller and pan and walks to me and wraps an arm around my waist, playfully yanking me to him and dips me a little. I reach for his shoulder with my arm not in the sling and let out a little yelp.

He looks down at me grinning. "My love, you swoon for me?" He leans down to kiss my lips while chuckling.

"Yes, I swoon, sugar bear." I drag out the word swoon and he starts to laugh harder as he moves his lips to my neck and with a final kiss, he brings us back up.

"Love, how about you don't call me sugar bear in front of any of those alpha males in your family. That can be your secret name for me. But in front of the guys, please refer to me as maybe, Thor, Hulk, The Hammer, Rock or Titanium."

On that last one, I crack up. "Titanium, huh? Titanium bear?"

I'm still laughing and so is he as he replies. "Yes, titanium. No bear."

"Titanium bear it is," I agree.

He grabs me and pulls me to him. "Love, if you ever call me those in front of the guys, I will turn you over my knee and spank you." he warns me.

Well, holy freaking heck and shit. My body freezes and I raise my eyes to meet his.

"I'm sorry, Jaycee. I wasn't thinking," he says as his expression turns serious. He brings his hands up and cups my face. He looks so scared. "I would never hurt you, Jaycee." he whispers.

Oh, that's why. "Well, I know that, Max. Of course, I know that." I roll my eyes.

"I felt you stiffen and then your face fell so I thought—" he starts but I interrupt him and look down to the floor before replying.

"No, when you said turn me over your knee and spank me..." my voice trails off.

"What?" he asks. I make nonessential mumbling noises. He lets out a deep chuckle and tries again. "What, Jaycee? My love?"

I still don't look up but I shuffle my feet and mumble again somehow managing to yell "spank" loud and clear. *UGH! Kill me now!*

"Jaycee, what are you trying to say?" When I don't respond, he leans into me. "You're saying you like the thought of me turning you over my knee and spanking that amazing ass of yours till it's as pink as this paint?" I fell my body jolt again. He's turning me on and I'm blushing red with heat and embarrassment but I don't say anything. "Good to know, love." He pulls me close and kisses me. When he pulls back, he's smirking, a dark promise evident in his gaze.

Damn!

He releases me and I turn around in a daze and start towards the window when I feel a stinging slap on my butt. I yelp and twist in surprise as my body flares with heat. With my mouth hanging open, I watch him as he kneels down and begins pouring paint into the pan. He glances up and winks at me then grabs his roller and paint and walks over to the wall to begin painting.

Hoy, boy!

Max is halfway through painting the room when Nash comes in and tells us that our grandma, Aunt Paige and Aunt Savannah brought food and they're setting it up kitchen. Max and I clean up the area a little and then head downstairs.

Pizza, wings and salad are spread across the kitchen island when we enter. My grandma and Aunt

Savannah are fixing drinks for everyone and setting out salad dressings. We turn as Violet comes in the front door helping Abigail make her way through the house and into the kitchen.

"Pizza! Just in time!" my sister almost screams, grinning widely. She sees us heading outside and hops towards the back door. In her excitement, she loses her balance, almost falling. Everyone in the room jolts and reaches out to catch her and my dad rushes over. Before he can get to her, she regains her balance. Leave it to my sister to do something to help break the somber mood everyone is in. That girl is so clumsy.

"For shit's sake, Abigail. You almost gave me a heart attack," dad yells. "You still have stitches and could have torn them. Be careful."

"Woah. Sorry, Daddy-o but it's pizza, and who is shit?" she asks, feigning honest curiosity.

"What?" my dad barks back and glares at her, ignoring the laughing and cursing going on around him.

"Shit. Who is this shit person who gives a sake?" She tilts her head still looking at him but trying not to laugh.

"Abigail," he warns. "Honest to Damien's creek, I'm going to bust your..."

"Okay," Bradley interrupts by clapping. "Pizza anyone?"

"Damien's creek? Where—?" Abigail goes on

poking the bear.

We all burst out laughing as Jake shakes his head and puts his plate back down on the counter. He walks over to Abigail, takes her crutches and hands them to Violet. He gently picks her up and walks to the door, opens it with one hand, then takes her outside and sits her on a chair. "Just sit here and behave yourself," he warns.

She gives him a big smack and pat on the cheek. "Will do. Thanks, king bro." She puts her hands in her lap and smiles back up at him sweetly.

Everyone laughs when he ruffles her hair to the point she looks like she stuck her finger in a light socket. "Anytime, runt."

She glares at him while fixing her hair, but she can't hide the love she has for him and the tiny smile playing at her lips.

"Pain killers. That's why we were late. I forgot her medicine and she was starting to feel some discomfort so I swung by the house and picked them up. She took some right as we left. Guess they kicked in." Violet tells us. My dad grumbles, but only because he's trying to hold back from laughing.

I start making my plate and grab an extra for Abigail and make hers. Max gets us some forks and napkins and we walk out to the patio and take our seats. I reach over and slide Abigail her plate and we both smile our secret sister smile. The one that conveys "nice work." It's the one that we save for driving the men in our life's crazy.

We all sit, join hands and say grace as Violet, Aunt Savannah and Grandma walk back in the house. Aunt Paige is walking around handing out napkins and asking if she can get anyone else anything. Everyone can tell she's nervous and is not sure what to do with herself. Uncle Brock drops his plate to the table and then reaches out and grabs her. She squeals as he pulls her into his lap and turns looking at him with her eyes bugging out.

"Brock, what in the world?" She tries to stand but he pulls her closer.

"It's going to be okay, sweetheart." He pushes her hair off her shoulder and turns her face to his. "I'm scared too but we're going to be okay. We've waited a long time to have a family and now, you, me and Callie," he smiles, "we're going to be one."

She smiles back and leans down and gives him a kiss. They forget for a few minutes that we're here because Uncle Brock starts to deepen the kiss when she suddenly pulls back and squeals. She jumps off his lap and runs inside; embarrassed while my dad and Uncle Duke laugh.

"What?" Uncle Brock asks. "She's just embarrassed. She likes us to have privacy."

"Enjoy *any* moments for the next few hours because once you have a little one in the house, private moments will be rare." My dad advises, then he corrects himself. "Callie, once Callie is in the house."

My dad and Uncle Duke share a grin as they look at

my Uncle Brock who is now showing worry. He looks over his shoulder at the back at the door where his wife just ran off to and frowns.

"Don't worry. It doesn't last for long. You'll get your privacy back in about oh, say, eighteen years," my dad shares.

Instead of getting upset my uncle Brock gets a goofy grin on his face. He's not worried. He's finally going to be a daddy.

Over the next few hours, my dad sets up two huge fans from his construction company in Callie's room that will dry the paint faster. Furniture is put together, clothes are hung and put away, shelves are put up and toys and books are placed on them. Max and Uncle Duke are pulling up the last of the tape and folding the drop cloths as Chase and Jake put together Callie's dollhouse and place it in the corner. Jesse and Bradley have put together a beautiful canopy bed and my aunt Paige is making the bed with the sheets she just washed and pulled from the dryer while Aunt Savannah and Grandma hang some ivory lace priscilla curtains on the window. Connor and Nash arrive carrying some block letters they've painted bright yellow that spell out *Callie*. They grab their tools and walk over to the wall and begin to hang them. I'm standing back, next to Violet and Abigail taking all this in. I flashback to the day at the lake, the day my grandpa collapsed. The day I thought was the beginning of the end of us. How worried I was about our family drifting apart. Worried the good times were over. I was wrong. We didn't drift apart. We pulled together. I didn't think we could ever surpass the joy from our childhood's and the memories we'd made. Yet, here we are, together, in this beautiful moment, making more joyous memories.

When we make it back home, Max and I say our goodnights and head to our room as grandma turns off the lights in the front rooms.

Max pulls me to sit next to him on the bench at the end of my bed, his forearms to his thighs and his head turned towards me. "So, you know I have to head back to work the day after tomorrow, right?"

I nod. "Yes, I know." I give him a forced smile. He doesn't smile back. I know he's concerned about leaving me but now that the threat is gone we need to get back to our lives

"I'm going to go down and talk with my manager, Nora Lee, and see if I still have a job." I reach over and smooth back his hair. He's going to have to shave off the goatee and get a haircut now that he's going back to work. I'm going to miss that goatee. "If I do, I'm hoping she'll start me back right away. I need things to get back to normal. I need a routine." He gives me a small smile. "Max, you need to get back to your patients, too." He takes a deep breath and releases it before agreeing.

"I know. I know." He stands up and walks to his bag and pulls out some gym shorts. "I'm going to get ready for bed. Do you want the bathroom first?" He asks as he throws his things over his shoulder.

"Go on, sugar." I call to his back and he turns slightly. I can see him grin but I ignore it as I glance back at his gym bag. "I'm going to find something to wear too." I tell him. I get up and walk to the chest of drawer and pull out what clothes I have in there. I walk over and place them on my bed as I open my dresser drawers and begin rearranging my clothes so I can fit the others in there. I then walk over to Max's gym back and pull out what clothes he has and walk over and begin placing them in the chest of drawers. Max pops his head out of the bathroom to watch me. I spend the next few minutes reorganizing our clothes with a smile on my face and my heart feeling warm.

Max walks up behind me and wraps one arm around my chest, pulling me to him. He moves my hair back off my neck and rests his chin there. "You sure?"

I reach up and touch his face. "More than sure, Max." Then self-doubt creeps in. "I mean you don't have to. I want you to be sure and I just thought..." I start to pull from him but he stops me and tightens his grip.

"Stop, love, I more than want to," he tells me as he kisses my neck up and down with his tongue gently tasting me. "We can go to my place tomorrow so I can grab some more of my stuff." He says and pulls his head back and turns me to face him. "I told you I was staying. You can't get rid of me." He lowers his head and kisses me, gently nipping my lips. I open my mouth for him but he only goes in for a second and then he's biting me softly. When he finally pulls back, my eyes stay closed and I feel like I'm in a trance.

"How's your shoulder?" he asks as he pulls the sling off my shoulder.

Mmmmhmm," is my only reply as I feel him pull my shirt off.

"Looks almost healed. A couple of more days and you won't have to wear the sling," he says as he undoes the front clasp on my bra.

"Yay!" I whisper yell. I lean forward and kiss his neck and feel his body shaking with laughter.

"Sugar bear, you going to stop talking now and you know, take care of business?" I ask against his neck.

"Jaycee, take the rest of your clothes off," his command is soft and low.

I start taking off my shoes and then my jeans. He's not making a move to take off anything. He's just stands watching me as I slowly remove my clothing, watching my movements and taking in my body. Once I get everything off, he turns me to face the bed.

"Bend over, love. Cheek and palms to the mattress. Ass in the air." He leans against my back and whispers in my ear.

Flip me over cause I'm done on this side, I'm about to faint, my breathing is so unsteady. My body feels like it's been hit by lightning. I step closer to the bed and do as he says. I can feel his heat behind me. He's fully clothed and that's turning me on big time too.

"Jaycee, you look beautiful," he moans.

I let out a whimper and tense in anticipation as his finger finds me. His body jerks and he moans when he feels how wet I am.

He starts moving his finger up and down spreading my wetness before he enters me and pushes in and out. Just one and it's driving me crazy. His hand leaves me for a moment and then I feel his jean covered legs push up against me from behind as he leans over me and starts feathering his fingers up and down my back and down to my ass.

"You can call me sugar bear in here, that's fine, but here's what happens when you call me that anywhere else." I sense him stand as the palms of his hands rest on top of my ass and he begins to softly massage me. Lost in the feeling, I'm not prepared for what comes next. *Slap.* My body jolts in surprise and then I moan because it feels so good. Before I can stop myself, I push back into him.

"Yes!" I cry out as he leans back down to my ear.

"You like that, Jaycee?" I nod and let out another moan when I feel him push up against me and I feel how hard he is. He slaps the other side and my body jolts back into him again. "More?" he asks and before I can answer I feel another slap. "Your ass is turning nice and pink for me," he says absently as his hands trail across the marks he's leaving.

"Yes, Max. More." I beg, rewarded with another smack. Now I'm wiggling around and pushing back into him. He smacks me one more time and then rubs the sting. I feel his finger glide down and push into me. I'm pulsing

46

and my body convulses when his finger enters me and I let out a cry of pleasure and start pleading. "Please, Max, now. I'm going to come."

He slowly pulls his finger from me and I let out another moan but one of displeasure from losing his touch. He finally picks up on my desperation and yanks off his shirt and jeans, positioning himself behind me again. He's hard and I moan as he rubs his tip through my wetness, coating himself. I feel another smack and then another on the other side.

"Spread your legs more for me, Jaycee," his voice sounds hoarse. I do as he says, feeling him line himself up at my entrance and in one strong powerful thrust, he's fully in me. I start to raise up as I let out a long moan but he puts a hand to my neck and pushes me back down and starts pumping inside of me. Oh, my God, yes. This is what I need. In between thrusts, he gives me a few more smacks which cause me to moan and push back into him and this time he lets me.

"Fuck, you're going to have to hurry. I won't last long. Touch yourself," he says orders me.

I reach down and touch myself. Rolling the tips of my fingers in circles, like he does. He has one hand on my hip pulling me back to him and the other is on my back holding me down. He starts to gain speed.

"Hurry, love," he grunts slapping me again and again until I explode. He grabs me by both hips, his fingers gripping me. He starts slowing down, his thrusts start going deeper causing my orgasm to drag out for what felt like forever. Exhausted, my upper body drops to the bed as he continues his long, deep thrusts.

"Beautiful, Jaycee," he moans and it sounds like he's in pain. He wraps his hand in my hair and pulls it tight. Just a touch of sting as he pulls my head back. I can't help but moan, loving his dominance and I show my surrender. When I do, and lift my hips to give him deeper access he slams into me.

"Shit, Jaycee. That's it." After a few more thrusts, he slams into me and then stops. "Fuck, I'm coming," he pants. The hand on my hair tightens along with the one on my hip. So tight I can't move. He stills and after a few seconds I feel his breathing start to slow. He keeps me like this for a few moments and then releases me to drops down on top of me. He gives me a few more thrusts which I return. I can feel our muscles still pulsing. We both lay still until finally, both our breathing returns to normal. I'm so relaxed and spent after that, I could fall asleep right here, like this.

As I lay there drifting, I think about what we just did and how much I loved it, how much I trust Max. How I wasn't scared of being spanked or his hand in my hair. How good it felt. I love Max. He would never hurt me. I mean like, I really liked this and I can't wait to do it again. At the same time a smile starts to form on my face the past rears it's ugly head again and I panic. Not out of fear, but shame and doubt.

Oh, my God. Will Max think I gave Rocky mixed signals? Because it wasn't like that. I'm not like that. Not with Rocky. He's going to think I'm some kind of creep that enjoys being hit. Then my craziness takes a different direction. *Wait.* He did that really well. He knew what he was doing. Has he done that to other women? My sanity stands ready to take a flying leap into the dark abyss for the insane, but halts when Max calls my name.

"Jaycee, What the hell is going on in your head?" He pulls his hand from my hair and smooths it back so he can see the side of my face. "Did I hurt you?" He stands and helps me up. "Stay here. I'll be right back." He walks into the bathroom and I hear the water turn on and then off. He comes back in with a washcloth and pushes me back on the bed and starts to open my legs but now I'm mortified, so I stop him and reach for the washcloth.

"I can do it," I whisper ashamed and worried.

He watches me as I turn away from him and then clean myself. I start to get up to put the cloth in the hamper and escape but he's not going to let me get away.

"Stop it, Jaycee." He takes the washcloth and tosses it in the bathroom and I watch it land on the floor. He lays down next to me and pulls me to him so we're face to face. "You're scaring the fuck out of me right now. Please talk to me," he begs.

I finally look over at him; his eyebrows are drawn together and he's frowning. I look away but he pulls my face back to him.

"Jaycee, I'm sorry. I shouldn't have done all that. I've never ever done that before. I shouldn't have been so rough. Please, look at me," he says softly.

"You've never done that before?" I ask and he shakes his head. "I thought maybe you'd done it before because you did it so…" I look away again, too embarrassed to finish. He pulls me back again still looking at me for an explanation. He knows I'm not telling him everything. "Max, I don't want you to think I'm a freak." I feel his body give a soft jerk and he puts his arms around me and pulls me close but doesn't say anything, letting me continue. "I really liked it all, Max. It was hot," I say softly. His arms spasms but his body starts to relax. "I'm not sure why I wasn't scared and of course you didn't hurt me, but I was completely into you and what we were doing and I wanted more. I just don't want you to think I like being hit, like you know, he did." My words trail off and I bury my face into his chest.

"Love, look at me, please," he calls as he puts his hand to my cheek pulling my face to his. "I've never done the stuff I've done with you." He smiles. "I want to do everything with you, experience new things with you and you only. I want to share these moments with someone I love and trust. Someone who doesn't judge me, too. Nothing about Rocky crossed my mind, I didn't feel any get mixed signals. I'm sorry you did. Let's not taint what we just shared with those memories," he leans down and puts his mouth to mine kisses me softly. "This was ours." he kisses me softly again. "And I liked it all too."

I look back at him, still in doubt and when I see his smile flash dimples, I finally start to relax.

"So I guess maybe we're both freaks? And I'm glad."

He kisses me again and says against my lips, "I love you so much, Jaycee. Forever and a day."

With my head on his chest and my eyes closing I sleepily whisper, "Love you too, Max. Forever and a day." I fall asleep with a smile on my face.

CHAPTER FIVE

The next morning, Max wakes me up to tell me he's going for a run and he'll be back in about an hour. I grab cup of coffee and walk out to the front porch where I see my grandma sitting on her rocker while she sews a button back on a shirt. I roll my eyes, most likely Jesse's button. I notice there's a chill in the air and I see she has a shawl around her. I walk back in the house and grab a throw blanket off the couch and wrap myself in it before rejoining her. I sit my coffee down and get situated on the porch swing before taking that first glorious sip.

"Hey, honey," she looks up and smiles as she pulls the needle through button hole.

"Hey, Grandma." I take a few more sips of coffee as I keep watching her in awe.

Sewing is not something I do or something I don't do well. I can sew a button on. That's about it and even when I do that, there's usually a gigantic wad of thread behind the button. Nothing but a tangle of thread but that button won't be going anywhere for a while that's for sure.

"So what you doing today, Grandma?" I ask, while still watching her.

She pulls the needle through a couple more times and then grabs a tiny pair of scissors and cuts the thread.

She puts the needle into her apple pin cushion and lays the shirt across the arm of her chair and starts rocking.

"Me and some of the other ladies are going to help out with the mother's day out program at church by watching the children and then I think I'm going to stop by Brock and Paige's to see how Callie adjusting. I know they want to give her a few days to get situated before they begin introducing her to everyone as a group. One-by-one, she'll probably do okay. Just want to be cautious not overwhelm her. Where she came from, with just her aunt, and her mom coming and going..." grandma shakes her head. "Having so many people around giving constant attention could either scare her or she'll soak it up like a sponge. They want to have a get-together this Saturday. Just something relaxing and laid back. She's a sweetheart and has really taken to Brock and Paige. She even calls them Mommy and Daddy which really surprised them. They started to talk to her about it but the social worker said she may not totally understand what she's saying and just to give it time. But from the way she looks at them, she could call them anything and it would be love. She's a happy little girl. Her life before, someone loved her. Not sure what happened to bring her to us but not going to question the blessing."

My heart breaks for what little Cole went through and whatever Callie must be going through now. I can't wait to meet her. We share a smile because we know they're all so deserving of each other. This beautiful little girl blessing their lives after the loss of Cole and them blessing her life with all the love they have.

I look up when I hear a noise and see Max coming up the drive from his run. He's sweaty and looks hot. I keep my eyes on him as he slows down and rests his hands on his knees and takes a few deep breaths before raising his shirt and wiping the sweat from his face. As he starts stretching a car turns into our drive.

At first I don't recognize it. But the more it comes into view, I remember it. It's Captain Walters and Sergeant Taylor's police vehicle. I freeze as I watch them exit the car.

Max, makes his way over to them and at the same time Grandma gets up and walks over to me and puts her hand to my shoulder.

"Honey, I'm sure everything is fine." The concern on her face betrays her words.

I turn back to them and like they sense my anxiety, they all look at me. I watch as Max climbs the steps with Sergeant Taylor and Captain Walters slowly following behind. Waiting for someone to say something has my heart feeling like it's about to burst from my chest.

"What's happened? Did they find Rocky?" I blurt out, needing to end this chapter of my life but Max shakes his head.

"They have news. It's about Rocky's dad. Dr. Jennings." He pulls me up and to his side. "Let's go inside."

Before heading inside, I approach Captain Walters and Sergeant Taylor, the sadness on their faces tugging at me. I don't know what's going on, but I know I owe them my life and I consider them part of my family now.

"Hey y'all." Sergeant Taylor gives me a short but strong hug and then I walk down to Captain Walters and put my arm around his waist and he draws me in close and holds me for a few moments.

"Hey, Jaycee. You look good." He pulls me back and looks down to me. "Just some news we thought you should know. Everything is okay."

I give a small smile and turn and walk back into the house.

We all sit in the living room. Max and I on the couch and my grandma in her chair as Captain Walters chooses to stand while Sergeant Taylor sits down on the straight back chair.

Finally, not able to hold it in, I bust out rambling with questions. "Okay, y'all are freaking me out. What's going on? Did you find Rocky? Is everyone okay?" I ask while looking back and forth between the two of them.

"No, Jaycee. We didn't find his body. They gave up the search. I'm sorry. We really wanted to give you and his family closure, but, no, that's not why we're here. What we wanted to talk to you about is probably going to shock you. It shocked us." They share a glance as I continue to sit and wait.

"We recently received some information from an anonymous source. It contained more information into the life Rocky was leading and more so, why. The source named quite a few people that were involved in drug production and there's a full investigation underway right now. It's bigger than we realized. One of the main figures in this is or was Dr. Jennings'."

I jerk at the news, not understanding what's going they're saying.

Sergeant Taylor continues. "Apparently, Rocky was taking his orders from him. He's the one who had Rocky doing his dirty work since his return from the military. This investigation has taken a one-eighty. Nothing is what it seemed. We think this runs deep in and around the area and into Mexico. We're hearing it wasn't street drugs, like cocaine and meth, being sold but a new drug. A drug Dr. Jennings was trying to develop along with others. Dr. Jennings wanted to be the next Timothy Leary or something. His position in the hospital gave him access to information and people that he reached out to. He brought them in as benefactors and supporters with the promise of fame. He wanted to reach legendary status and begin developing a new drug. It involves some of our local city government and judges. Elected officials he held in his pocket. That's how he was able to arrange a midnight bail hearing for Rocky the night he was released," he finishes.

They've stopped talking and are waiting for a reaction from but I'm dumbfounded. When I finally speak, it's to confirm what I think they're saying.

"So, you're telling me Dr. Jennings', Rocky's dad is some type of drug manufacturer? Mad scientist? He may have judges in his pocket?" I ask.

"The worst part, Jaycee, we think he was blackmailing Rocky into doing what he wanted by threatening to harm his mom and brother, Lina and Lincoln Jennings." Captain Walters informs me.

I start thinking back and I remember something Rocky said to Linc that day in the cabin. *"You know what's funny, Linc? She thinks I'm a monster, the devil himself. But she should really get to know our dad..."* My eyes start to water as I remember the night Kelly crashed in yelling during dinner. Dr. Jennings was the one Rocky kept looking to and waiting on for orders. Oh, my God!

"But, Linc. How did Linc get away? Why did he keep Rocky but not Linc?" I ask in confusion.

Captain Walters looks down and shakes his head. "Listen, Rocky, no matter what we tell you, the things he did to you, they were wrong, criminal. He hurt people. No two ways about that, but after talking to Linc and Lina Jennings, it seems Rocky may have sacrificed himself in some way. Taking the brunt of abuse and such from Dr. Jennings so his brother and mother could be free. They didn't know any of this information, but things are starting to make sense. Like with you, right now. Puzzle pieces are starting to fit."

I sit still taking all this in and it hits me. "Dr. Jennings? Where is he? Did the police pick him up? I mean, he's going to pay, right?" my voice raises; full of anger.

My grandma chimes in. "He'll spend time in jail, right, detectives?"

"Jaycee, Dr. Jennings was found in his office this

morning, dead. Murdered. Someone unloaded an entire clip from a 9mm into him and the house had been torn apart. Someone was looking for something," Captain Walters says. I sit back hard against the couch in shock, my mouth falling open.

"What the hell?" Max yells.

"That's all we know now." Captain Walters tells him.

I get up and start to pace as Max and Grandma sit in shock.

"He's dead?" I wait for their nod of confirmation. "So if Kelly and Rocky are both dead...I mean, who?" I ask and start to pace again.

Max pulls me to him and holds me, whispering in my ear. "Love, calm down."

I turn on Max. "NO! I won't calm down. Listen, I get it. Rocky was bad. I know firsthand how bad and he doesn't get a free pass. He hurt my sister and me. He hurt others. He paid the ultimate price for his sins. But, his dad? I mean, he abused Rocky and Linc, their mom. And he's dead? He doesn't pay? Who killed him?" I demand, livid.

Max stands and puts his hand to my shoulder and one to my cheek. "Jaycee, he probably knew too much. If what the detectives are saying is correct and this runs deep as they think, someone probably took him out before he could talk," Max tells me as he caresses my cheek and smooths my hair, trying to calm me.

Captain Walters speaks up. "That's the theory. Someone was nervous about him making a deal and releasing names and eliminated the threat. There was no forced entry and he was found at his desk wearing his glasses. We think whoever it was, he knew and didn't consider them a threat," he adds.

Captain Walters stands and walks to me. "Jaycee, the main reason we came is because this is about to hit the media and it's going to be a feeding frenzy. You and your sister, your names were never released to the public under victim anonymity protection so you'll be okay but we just didn't want you to be blindsided by all of this. Lina and Linc Jennings along with Nick Callaghan are supposed to heading back to Lubbock soon, but I have a feeling they're not going to be so lucky. I know your sister and Nick are close and you speak to Mrs. Jennings so we just want y'all to be careful."

Huh? What? I knew it! Nick and Abigail are more than friends. I look at Max who just shrugs his shoulders. I knew the night at the hospital when he came rushing down the hallway to her room and her waking up and asking for him something was up. I guess I'll have to talk to her about all that later.

"Okay. Well, thank you both for letting us know." I move closer to Max, confusion following me.

"Yes, thank you for stopping by," my grandma comes over and shakes both their hands and excuses herself.

I know what she's doing, she's calling my dad and

59

uncles.

"Okay. I'm okay," I say and look at Max and then Sergeant Taylor and Captain Walters. "I mean, I'm shocked, but I'm okay," I clarify after seeing their doubtful glances.

Captain Walters walks up to me, pulls me into a hug and whispers on top of my head, "Jaycee, there is going to be an end to all this. You'll see. Soon." He walks to the door and waits.

Sergeant Taylor walks up, touches me on the arm. "We'll be in touch." Max walks them out to the front porch, and they shake hands and say their goodbyes.

"You okay, love?" he asks as pulls me to sit down with him on the sofa. "Jaycee, just like they said, there will be an end." He takes my hand and squeezes it. and takes a deep breath. "Maybe, with you or because of you, he wanted to do better, be better but it was just too late. He didn't know how or didn't have any good left." Max tells me and pulls me to sit in his lap. "You bring that out in people. The good. People want to try." He leans his forehead on mine. "Let him rest in peace with that, okay, love?"

"Okay, Max." His words make sense to me. On some level, I know it's the truth; but I just don't have forgiveness in me for Rocky yet. Maybe in time, but right now, he's still the monster in my worst nightmare.

"I have to head over to my place to pick up some of my stuff and then I'm going by to see my parents. You want to go with me?" he looks nervous while waiting for my answer. "I mean I know you said you need to go by work, but after?"

I smile because I'd love that. "Yes. Let me get showered. I'll hurry." I jump up and start towards our room

"Okay, take your time. I'm calling my mom to let her know we're coming."

"Okay, sugar bear," I call back and I hear him chuckle. I start to laugh as I grab a couple of towels and head to the shower.

CHAPTER SIX

On the way to Max's place, we stop at Dan's Grocer so I can speak to Nora Lee, my supervisor. When we walk through the doors I realize how much I miss my job, and my co-workers. I hear my name being called and I look over and see Bernice walking over to me. She pulls me into a hug as she apologizes.

"I'm so sorry, Jaycee. I should have called the police or your family, something." The agony in her voice twists my heart. She steps back and looks down. "I knew in my gut something was wrong and I just..." I stop her.

"Bernice, you couldn't have known," I say to try and make her feel better. "So please, don't blame yourself at all, okay?" I pull her back into a hug.

"Jaycee!" I look up to see a few more of my co-workers who don't have any customers walking towards me with big smiles.

"Hi, y'all!" I greet them as one by one they give me hugs. I take a moment to introduce them to Max. "Rachel, Trish, Kim, Debra, Naomi, Ezzat, Amalia, Sylvia, Ralph, Christopher, Nathan, Joey, Mary Joyce, Annette, Dora, Amber and Ryan." I gesture to Max. "This is Max "Blue" Bradshaw." He walks forward and shakes each of their hands.

"Please, call me Blue." I feel him tap me on my butt with his hand and I can't help but smile.

"Jaycee?" My name is called from behind me and I know the voice immediately.

Nora Lee is one tough cookie. When I first started working here, her no nonsense personality put me off, but now I find its just part of who she is. I can tell she cares about her workers probably more than just a boss should. Anyway, despite her best efforts to keep people at bay by her outer toughness, I've grown to love her. I call her sunshine which she thinks is hilarious so when I turn around and see her I can't help it.

"Sunshine!" I call out and start towards her. She smiles back but her lip wobbles and her eyes water. She pulls me into a hug.

"Jaycee, oh, I'm so glad to see you and that you're okay. I've been sending up prayers for you and your family." I hug her and then we step back.

"Well, God heard you because I'm doing great."

"Of course He heard me." She scoffs, dragging me towards her office. "Y'all, get back to work and start breaks. Look at the clipboard, your break times are written down." she calls over her shoulder. A round of "Yes ma'am" from my co-workers can be heard as we walk to her office. She takes her seat behind her desk and waits for us to sit across from her.

"Nora Lee, this is Max, or Blue I should say. He goes by Blue." He reaches out to shake her hand

"Hi, Ms. Nora Lee." She smiles and even blushes which makes me giggle silently because that's something new.

"Hello, Blue," she says as she collects herself. After a second she turns to me. "So, Jaycee. You ready to come back to us? To go back on the schedule?" she asks.

I sigh in relief. I didn't know if it was going to be a problem. I look at her with gratitude. "I'm so ready, Ms. Nora Lee. You have no idea. Thank you for waiting for me," I say and she smiles but it quickly fades.

"Well, it wasn't really my decision. The owners, Dean and Barbie Norris, wanted to wait. You're a good worker and what happened wasn't your fault. We all just want you to get better. You'll always have a place here." With that news, my eyes water.

"Thank you and please, let me them know how grateful I am."

"I will, Jaycee. Now, when can you start back up and do you have any restrictions?" She asks and after a short discussion, I get my schedule and we say our goodbyes.

I'll be heading back to work in the morning.

About twenty minutes later, we pull up in front of a huge one story brick home. Max gets out of the car and walks around and opens my door, reaching for my hand. I take it and let him pull me out.

"Is this your house, Max?" I ask, studying the brick

building.

He looks back at the house. "No. It's my parents'." He pulls me to his side and we start towards the front door. "There's a duplex around back. I've been staying between there, the barracks or the hospital. I haven't really settled into one place but this was closest since coming home from my last tour."

I start to panic. I was going to ask him questions about his parents. Get a feel for how or what I should do. I start to pull from him when he looks back to me in question. "Max, I wasn't ready," I whisper and I watch as he grins. "I thought we were going to your place and then I was going to ask you a gazillion questions so I'd be ready to meet them."

He starts laughing. "A gazillion? Love, that's a lot of questions." I nod jerkily.

"Okay, so here. Let me give you the short version. My dad is prior military and grew up on a farm in the mid-west. He's your typical average guy. My mom grew up in the Philippines and she misses it a lot. She can talk your ear off about her home. She loves to cook, and well, the minute we walk in the door, she'll start asking if we're hungry and whether we say we are or aren't, she'll start cooking a huge meal. I always just say I'm hungry because it makes her happy to cook. Both my parents are what I call," he pauses a moment. "Hippies." He crinkles his forehead in thought. "Yes, that's a good name for them. Hippies."

Hippies? Okay, so now I'm still worried but also

hopeful.

"Um, they grow most of their own food and..." he stops short when a woman with an accent yells his name.

"Maxwell!"

I slowly turn around and I see the prettiest petite Asian woman smiling back at Max with huge dimples. His mom.

"Oh, my God, Maxwell," she gushes as she hugs him and then turns to me; her smile vanishing. "This is Jaycee?" She's staring at me and pointing but obviously talking to Max.

I look at Max who walks to my side and puts his arm around my shoulder and smiles at me which finally has me relaxing a little bit. I smile back but when I look back to her she's still staring me down. *Shit!*

"Hi, ummm, Mrs. Bradshaw. It's nice to meet you," I say and she stands up straight and I finally notice she's wearing camouflage pants with a black sweater and wedges with at least a three-inch heel. She's stunning. She has long, almost black hair, falls down to the middle of her back, dark brown eyes and the same olive skin as Max. She's wearing a lot of gold jewelry. I'm not sure about this fashion working for everyone, but it's sure working for her.

She walks up and cups my cheek and finally speaks. "I'm sorry for what happened to you. He's dead?" I nod. "Good. Forgive him and let God deal with him." She steps closer to me. "I was briefly married before their dad. He wasn't a kind man; he cheated and he hurt me. One night,

I'd had enough, I found my courage, the strength that he tried so hard to steal from me. I knocked him on the head with a piece of wood and when he dropped, I grabbed my things and ran home to my parents."

Her admission shocks me, but I'm grateful for her acceptance and for her sharing her story so bravely. She starts pulling me to the house. "Next thing I heard, he was dead." I almost fall down when she says that. "My home was just like here, years ago police didn't get involved in domestic fights. Thank God it's not like that anymore. Men can't hit their wives and kids and then pay off the police with a bottle of whiskey, money or claiming they're protected through their religion. But even so, then and now? You still need to learn how to take care of yourself. I did and so did you when you had to." She smiles and turns back to the door and opens it. Max takes it from her and holds it for us to walk in. I freeze when I walk in the house. It's like walking into the orient.

Max speaks up. "She decorated like they do in the Philippines. Lots of reds and dark woods."

I look up to him. "It's beautiful, Max." I turn to his mom and she's smiling at him. "You have a beautiful home, Mrs. Bradshaw," I tell her, still looking around.

She walks around the counter to the fridge and starts pulling food out. "Thank you, Jaycee. Now, are you hungry?" She asks as she grabs pots from the cupboards. "Because I'm going to cook. So, sit. We're going to eat."

Max and I sit on stools at the breakfast counter watching his mom cook. He wasn't exaggerating. She has a pan on every burner and something warming in the microwave. He's smiling with dimples on full display and all of a sudden I'm feeling shy. I start to look away when Max's mom calls out loudly.

"HONEY!" she yells. I almost fall off my stool in surprise and Max starts cracking up.

"Ay Naku. Jaycee! Sorry," she says and she starts giggling. "Ihinto ang tumatawa o kukunin ko na pop mo sa ulo," she says and turns back to the stove still giggling.

I raise my eyebrows at Max in bewilderment. "She just told me to stop laughing or she's going to beat me," he tells me.

His mom whips back around with the spatula in her hand and points it at him.

"Ay Naku, Maxwell" she says scolding him.

Max sits up straight and tells his mom, "Okay. Okay, Mom."

The back door opens and in walks a slightly younger version of Max only much more rough looking. Scary but handsome. He's just as tall and his frame is only slightly leaner. He's wearing a uniform and it takes me a second to see the emblem on his shirt. He's S.W.A.T. Holy heck! He's wearing black, tactile-looking clothing, combat boots and he's sporting a holster with a gun. His hair is much longer than Max's and he has a goatee.

He walks up to Max's mom and leans down and gives her a kiss on the head.

"Hey, Mom. Whatcha cooking?" he asks.

He looks over at me and winks and Max stands to meet him halfway when he starts toward us.

"Hey, brother!" Max says and gives him a man hug.

"Hey, Blue. You look good, brother," he tells Max and then looks back at me.

His eyes travel up and down me and I feel myself blush.

"Really, Johnny?" Max shakes his head and walks over to me, draping his arm around my shoulder.

"Jaycee, this is my little brother, Johnny," Max says.

Before I can say anything, Johnny walks over to me and takes my hand and leans into me. "Hi, Jaycee. It's nice to finally meet you after all these years."

Johnny takes a seat at the table and continues to speak.

"You have no idea what you've put me through," Johnny says as he leans back in the chair. "My brother here," he flips his thumb over at Max while keeping his eyes to me. "Used to walk around the house singing tragic, soul wrenching sad love songs because of you. It was not only pathetic but he sounded like a dying cat. It was awful." He looks at Max and shakes his head. "Have you played her any of the songs you wrote for her?"

I feel Max tense beside me.

"Johnny, really? You can shut up now." Max laughs

nervously.

"Oh, I could. But why would I?" Johnny says.

I can see his bright smile shining through his goatee; he's got dimples too, though not as deep as Max's.

"He had this one song, 'Why' and that's all he said the entire song, why, why, why, why," Johnny says in a singsong voice dragging out the last why. "He'd walk around strumming his guitar between two or three chords singing 'why' over and over."

Now I'm totally into this story. Max is turning red, but chuckling as his brother continues giving him the gears.

"After about the third day of him moping around singing his chart topping love song, 'Why,' my dad walked into his room and grabbed the guitar out of his hands and handed him a baseball bat. Told him to hit the batting cages. Took his guitar and locked it up in the gun safe," Johnny tells me.

I'm trying not to laugh but it's impossible. I can feel Max laughing next to me; his mom is doubled over laughing as she's trying to put the food from the pans onto plates.

"One more day of singing and that guitar was going to become kindling," a deep, husky voice says.

Turning towards the voice, a man is leaning in the doorway, regarding the scene with obvious amusement. I know immediately it's Max's dad and pause to take in his long blonde hair pulled back in a ponytail and full beard. He seems to be just a little taller than Max and Johnny;

70

muscular but leaner. He's wearing reading glasses perched on his nose and his blue eyes are looking at all of us over the rims. He's dressed almost the same as their mom, with camouflage pants only he's wearing a black t-shirt with his. Silver rings cover almost every finger and leather bracelets wind around each wrist accompanied by tattoos running up both arms.

Johnny and Max have dark hair and eyes like their mom and they also have her dimples. If I would never have seen this man, I'd think they were the spitting image of their mom but now that I see him, I see they look like their dad.

"Hey, Jaycee. I'm Acer," he says and walks over to me. "These two," and he gestures between Max and Johnny, "belong to me and their mother, Ana." I watch him glance over at that stove where their mom is still loading food onto plates. "I apologize. We truly did our best and yet they still came out the way they did." He grins and winks at me.

I start laughing along with Max and Johnny.

He straightens his features back to serious and looks at Max and Johnny, shaking his head before he walks over to their mom and looks at all the food. "Jesus, Ana. Did you cook everything in the icebox?" he asks in humor. He carries some plates over to the big dining room table and sets them down. "Get your lady something to drink, Blue. Johnny help your mom while I get something for us and grab the soy sauce and kimchi from the fridge," he says and starts setting the plates out.

71

We sit for the next hour talking about their garden, guns, the Philippines, my family and their family. I find out Max was born in Philippines and didn't really speak English the first few years of his life because he was mostly around his aunts and mom and they spoke in Tagalog. Now, like Johnny, they speak both. Max explains a little about what's been happening with me and the news of Dr. Jennings. Johnny chimes in, saying he's been hearing about everything through the grapevine at work and that it looks like it's going to become a huge local scandal.

After we say our goodbyes, we walk down a path behind their property to a building.

"We'll go in and I'll pack a few things, then I'll go back and grab the car and pull it around to load. Right now, I'll just show you around." As we start down the path, Max points out a garden. It has tomatoes, onions, peppers, carrots and herbs. I see a small area with rose bushes of different colors. "My dad, he loves to garden. He loves the outdoors. I know he left his small hometown to see the world but wherever we've been, he's always had a garden, like home. My mom, in the Philippines, she grew up on a farm also, coconuts and rice. Back at my grandparents, when my dad was away on deployments we stayed with them and it was pretty awesome. Rice grows in lowlands and coconut trees everywhere. The beach, Cebu, where she was born and raised, the water is crystal blue. It's so clear you can see to the bottom. Nothing like the beaches around here." As he talks, I can see him travel back in his mind. "One day I'll take you." He looks down at me smiling. "You can meet my family there and then I'll take you to meet my dad's family." I smile back up at him.

"I'd really like that, Max. I look forward to it," I say. He leans down and gives me a slow kiss. It's a kiss full of promise and I give back to him in my kiss with just as many promises.

We finally make it to a duplex towards the back of the property. It's fairly large and in the same red brick as the main house. He pulls keys from his pocket and unlocks the door and moves aside so I can walk in first. I'm hit with the same decorating theme. Lots of reds and dark wood. It's beautiful. He grabs me by the hand and starts pulling me deeper into the house.

"My parents built this a few years ago for guests. My mom and dad like their privacy but they also like having guests. When my dad's family visits they stay a week or two but when my mom's side comes for a visit, they can stay up to a few months," he explains. I think back to Bradley coming home for visits while my uncle Duke and Aunt Savannah were stationed overseas and he stayed for months at a time. It was the best of times having a house full. Max stops and opens another door and waits for me to walk inside. His bedroom. His guitar is off in the corner and I think back to Johnny and his teasing and I start laughing. Max groans as he walks over and sits on the edge of the bed with his head down.

"I'm never going to live that down, am I?" I giggle as I stand in front of him. "Max, I'm honored. But why, oh why, did you write and sing a song called why, and why about me, Max, why?" I ask and throw my head back in laughter when his face turns red, and his dimples pop out. He pulls me forward by my hips and I put my hands on his shoulders.

"Well, Jesse and I played football and soccer together and you use to come with Jake to watch him play." *He saw me?* Jake had already graduated but would still go and watch Jesse play and I would beg to tag along. I remember going but what he doesn't know, I only came for one reason—him. I'd watch him and afterwards he would usually walk over with Jesse and say hello to Jake not even sparing me a glance.

"If you're thinking I didn't see you, oh, I saw you. I always saw you," he shares. "After one practice, I'd had enough of waiting and I went to Jesse in the locker room. I asked if it would be okay to call you but Jake walked in. He overheard and nixed the whole idea." He sighs and rests his head on my stomach. I raise my hand and start rubbing my fingers through his hair. "I want to say he was wrong but he wasn't. He was right, about everything." He looks back up at me. "You were a freshman and no matter what happened or didn't happen between us, I was graduating and you would still be there three more years without me. When Jake pointed out that wasn't fair to you, it fucking broke me but I knew he was right. You were going to have parties and proms and then that fuckwad, Harry asked you out," he says his voice laced with anger.

I pull gently at Max's hair so he looks in my eyes. "Max, Harry was a concession prize and not much of one. The boy I dreamed of was you. But I thought you were so out of the realm of possibility I just moved on and went with what I thought was the next best thing."

He gives me a sad smile. "I know, Jaycee. I did the same thing." He pulls my left leg forward behind my knee to kneel beside him on the bed and then the other so I'm straddling him; his hands holding me to him. "When Jake laid it out for me all I could think was, why? Why did we have to be so far apart in age, so many why's," he says. I felt the same so I don't even smile as he raises his lips up to mine. "Fuck, love, I waited a long time for you."

I hold his head to mine as his hands slide up my back and into my hair and he grasps the strands. Holy heck. I love when he does that and I show him by grinding down on him and moaning. He opens his mouth even wider, trying to devour me and I let him. Next thing I know, his hands are out of my hair and under my shirt. I bring my hands down between us and try to unbutton his shirt but when I can't get to the buttons, I let out a frustrated groan. His hands come back to my hips as he stands and lowers my feet to the ground. I don't waste any time. I yank open his shirt and buttons go flying as I slam my mouth back down on his. I don't bother taking his shirt off. I run my nails down his chest to the waist of jeans and start undoing his belt as he's reaching down doing the same.

I get to him first and reach in to feel him. He's so thick and hard and the second his heat hits my hand I feel my body respond. My body knows and wants him. He pulls my hand away and turns to walk me backwards to the bed. He pushes me down and starts pulling off my shoes and then my jeans. When he has me down to my underwear, he pulls off his boots one by one and then comes down on top of me. I raise my legs and wrap them around his waist as he lifts us and scoots us all the way back to the pillows. I keep my legs tight around him as he pushes my hair from my face. I watch him as his eyes search my face and finally look at me in my eyes.

"Fuck, Jaycee, I can't believe you're actually here," he whispers and I give a small smile.

"Max. I love you. I've waited forever for you." He slowly leans down and starts kissing me again.

"Love, I need to marry you soon. I need to put my babies in you." he whispers in my ear. My eyes begin to water with happy tears. "I want our lives to finally start." He trails kisses down my neck. I keep my hands to his head and turn mine to give him better access. He stops at my shoulder where there's still an angry red welt from the bullet and kisses it. "So sorry I didn't get to you before he did that." He stops and leans his head down. "I am so fucking sorry."

I put my hand under his chin and raise his head so he'll look at me. "Max, you saved my life. The very breath from your lungs breathed life back into me. I'm only alive because of you." I say and pull him back to me. "Max, I need you inside of me." I lift my body up into his. "It hurts when you're not close. I feel empty and alone. Please," I whisper.

"I know, Jaycee. I hurt too," he says against my lips. His hand travels up to my lace covered breast and pulls the cup down and lowers his head to lick and suck on first one breast then the other.

"Max, please," I plead as he reaches behind me and undoes the clasp of my bra and yanks it down my arms, throwing it off to the side as I try pushing his shirt off his shoulders. His hand slips in my panties and his fingers find me.

"Max. God, please, now!" Before I realize what's happening, he leans up and uses both his hands to rips my panties off and pushes his jeans down.

"You're so hot, wet and ready. Legs up, now, love," he commands. I raise them up as he centers himself and pushes in on a long, strong thrust until he bottoms out. I look up at him and he's still wearing his shirt but it's hanging open. His jeans are lowered only enough to release himself. His strokes are hard, strong and slow with each movement. Every time he bottoms out, we groan. I grab at his shoulders, but he takes my hands and places them in his palms and then slides them up behind my head with our fingers laced together. His body has mine pinned and it feels wonderful. He brings his mouth back to mine and kisses me, our tongues tasting and then he travels down my neck and then back to my lips. I struggle against his hands only to feel his fingers tighten on mine.

He leans down and whispers in my ear, "Let me take care of you. Just feel me, Jaycee." He's rubbing his pelvic bone against me causing a delicious friction that has me raising up to get more. He tilts my hips to where I can feel him better and now instead of rubbing up and down, he grinds and I'm about to lose my mind. Our bodies, they're sweaty and close. The parts not clothed are gliding easily against each other. A few thrusts later my body feels and catches it as my world crashes into bliss. I see stars and I know I'm calling his name because he whispers in my ear, "I got you, Jaycee. Fuck, I got you. Let go."

A few seconds later he powers into me and finds his release. His groan is just as long and loud as mine. We lay there for a long time until he finally releases my hands. I run them under his damp shirt along his wet back and around to his chest. I wrap my hands around his neck and let my fingers slide into his damp hair. I can feel him kissing and licking my neck as his hand slides down my side, my ribs, over my hip bone and then down my leg where he pulls it up higher behind my knee and gives a couple more thrusts.

"Shit, Jaycee. I'm getting hard again," he moans.

I lift my hips up to him and start thrusting back and we both moan.

"More, Max," I beg. "Max, I feel like I'm going to die if you don't keep going," I whisper.

He sits back on his haunches, jeans now pushed down, and rips off his shirt. He comes forward and I help him kick his jeans off, using my feet. Once they're off, he kisses me hard and then lifts back up and grabs my legs behind my knees, pulling me up his thighs as he slams inside of me. *Yes.*

I squirm trying to get to him, to get closer, more,

deeper. I want to be one in every sense. My breathing becomes labored as I feel my release building again.

"Fuck, Jaycee. I don't want to hurt you but fuck I need to take you hard. I want what's finally fucking mine. You are mine, love." He slams into me and it's still not enough. "Fuck, tell me to stop if I hurt you but I'm going to go deep, Jaycee. You're going to feel me for days," he promises.

"Yes. Make me feel you." I beg.

He wraps his arms behind my knees and pushes them all the way back, coming down on top of me. His pace increases and his thrusts become more urgent as we each push each other towards finding our pleasure.

"Yes, Max. Oh, my God, that feels good," I whimper.

I start to feel it building again and he must too because he starts pounding in me even harder and I tighten around him to a point I didn't know was possible. I'm pretty sure I scream, but he keeps going and helps me ride it out. When my arms and legs collapse back to the bed, he flips me over on my belly and pulls me up by my hips and enters me from behind.

"Again, Jaycee," He demands.

Again?

"That's it, love," he says as he grabs my hips and slaps my ass.

"Max," I breath as he drags his hand up my back and grabs my hair and pulls my head back.

"Shit, Jaycee. Hurry. Touch yourself." I reach down and one touch is all it takes and I explode again before dropping to the mattress.

He lets go of my hair and brings both hands back to my hips as he powers into me a few more times before I hear him groan out a cuss and collapse on top of me. We lay like that for a while until he finally pulls free and I make a pained sound. I already want him back. I feel cold and empty as he lays down next to me and pulls me to him. I rest my head on his chest and drape my leg over his and that's the last thing I remember until I hear Max whisper my name and kiss my cheek.

"Hey, love. I let you sleep as long as I could but it's probably time we get back home," he says.

"I'm sorry. I didn't mean to fall asleep on you," I apologize.

"I guess I wore you out," he says with a grin.

"You can wear me out like that anytime, sugar bear." When I say that, he gives me full on dimpled smile.

"Good to know." He half jokes, giving me a slow soft peck on the lips.

"I'm going to go down and pull the car around. The bathroom is across the hall if you need it." he lets me know and with one last peck he gets up and walks out.

I get up and start looking around the room for my clothes and when I pick up my torn panties, I smile. The front door closes just as a phone starts ringing. I quickly put on my bra; it's not my cell phone, I know that from the ringtone, I spot Max's on the nightstand and move quickly to try and catch the call. It stops as I grab it, but I see the name Kim flash across the screen. I tug my jeans on commando and I'm about to button them when it starts to ring again. I'm not sure what to do, but I'm guessing I should probably answer it. He was just talking about getting married and having a family. I'm pretty sure I don't have anything to worry about, but my heart's still beating fast and hard. I pick up the phone and slide my finger across the screen and answer.

"Hello?"

"Oh, I'm sorry. I was looking for Blue. I must have dialed the wrong number. Sorry." Before she can hang up, I quickly respond.

"No. This is Max's, uh, Blue's phone," I tell her and her voice changes.

"Okay. So who am I talking to?" she asks. Shit, not again.

"Um, I'm Jaycee," I say and hear her sigh.

"Aw, Jaycee. Blue finally got his girl. Well, I guess won't be seeing him around anymore," she says sadly.

I stay quiet, not sure what to say. A hand takes the phone from me; my eyes meet Max's troubled ones and my heart cracks a little. And here's where it goes bad, again. I'm never anyone's one and only. Is this how it always is?

Max's voice snaps me out of my daze. "Hey, Kim.

Sorry about that. I can explain," he says.

I find my shirt and pull it on as I turn to leave the room. I don't want to hear any of this. As I start to walk out, Max grabs my arm, and without thinking, I yank away from him. "Finish your conversation and then take me home, please."

I don't know why, but I don't stop walking. I walk right out the front door and up the path. I see Max's parents house and Johnny is outside standing next to his motorcycle working on something. He sees me and calls out but I don't acknowledge him.

"Hey, Jaycee. Wait up."

Johnny catches up and start keeping pace with me. "So, what did my big brother do?" he asks. "Did he sing 'Why?' for you? Because I'd need no further explanation," he tries to joke.

That's funny and a smile tries to form on my lips, but it can't. My eyes start to tear up so I pick up my pace. I just want to take off running.

"Jaycee. Hey, stop," Johnny pleads and takes a couple of steps in front of me. "Hey, sweetheart. Stop. You're not wearing shoes. You're going to hurt yourself. What the hell happened?" His voice is full of concern.

Shit, I didn't even notice I wasn't wearing shoes. I can't feel anything. I stop walking and look up at Johnny as the tears start to fall. "Kim happened," I say and he looks at me in confusion.

"Kim?" he asks.

I drop my face into my palms and start crying. "Yes, Kim. She called and he's talking to her right now. Is that his girlfriend?" I ask.

My name is bellowed and I look at Johnny and shake my head. I can't talk to him right now.

"Babe, listen to me," he says as he holds up his hand to stop Max. I can see out of the corner of my eye Max stops but he starts pacing. "Kim is not Blue's girlfriend. Blue has been in love with you since he was seventeen years old. He's never had a girlfriend." He pulls my hands from my face as he continues. "He's dated and a couple of times I thought maybe he was going to try and move on; but that never happened. He never brought them home. They never met our parents. He was too hung up on you. Kim was one of those he saw a couple of times. I talk to Blue every few days and he hasn't mentioned her or anyone in months so I don't know what happened—but what I do know is—Kim is not his girlfriend," he assures me.

There's truth and sincerity to what Johnny's saying, I see that when I look in his eyes. He glances over at Max and frowns. When I can finally bring myself to meet Max's stare, he looks like he's about to pull his hair out. I feel a twinge of guilt for running out as I hesitantly walk over to him; tears beginning to run down my face.

"You. Only you. You've always been it for me, Jaycee. I didn't mean to hurt you, or hurt her. She's always known about you, and where my heart truly was. That's

83

how she knew your name. I told her a long time ago when she questioned why I wouldn't take things to the next level with her. Jaycee. Plain and simple. Jaycee." he reaches out and pulls me to him. "Fuck, love, do not ever take off on me like that again," he pleads.

I slowly bring my arms up and wrap them around his neck and start bawling.

"Jesus, I'm sorry," he breathes against my ear.

He rests his cheek on my head and we just stand there on the side of the road. "Well, my work here is done." Johnny's voice sounds muffled as I'm still nestled in Max's arms.

I pull from his embrace. "Johnny, thank you," I call after him. He winks at me and gives Max a chin jerk.

"Hop up, Jayc." Max tells me and lifts me up by my butt. I wrap legs around his waist. "Let's go get your shoes and my stuff and go home, okay?" he asks. I lay my head down in his neck and nod. "I love you."

I still can't talk so I just nod. I'd rather die than lose Max and I felt like that's what was about to happen.

After we load up the car, we make our way back to my home. We haven't spoken much, but Max hasn't let go of my hand. He's had it in a tight grip the entire ride back.

After we unload, we go to our room and he starts putting his clothes away. He hangs a few uniforms and drops his boots in my closet. His shaving cream, deodorant, shampoos are now mixed in with mine and I have to say, I like it. It feels good. I'm starting to feel foolish for my earlier reaction to Kim. I should have trusted him. I should have talked to him. I catch him watching me when I finally decide to seek him out and apologize.

"I'm sorry, Jaycee," he says as he takes in a deep breath and slowly releases it. "I'm really sorry. I haven't heard from her in months. It didn't cross my mind to tell you about her. I didn't think I owed her an explanation, but I guess I did."

I swallow hard before responding. "I should have talked to you. Asked you. I'm sorry I reacted the way I did. I'm new at this and my track record? Well..." I say, ashamed.

He pulls me to him. "Jayc, As far as I'm concerned, nothing came before me and you. Let's just forget everyone but us and now. Move forward." We both know that's unrealistic by why not just give it a try?

"Sounds good, sugar bear," I tell him with a smile, watching his eyes become hooded at my term of endearment. "I guess we should get some sleep. Tomorrow, we both have to get back to work." I reach up on my tiptoes and give him a small peck on his lips.

I grab a gown and a pair of panties from my drawer and make my way to the bathroom to clean up. When I come out, I set the alarm on my phone and lay it on my nightstand and crawl into bed. Max heads into the bathroom, glancing at me to make sure I'm alright before closing the door. My eyes are closed and I'm half asleep by the time I feel the bed dip when he sits down on the edge. Finally, he lays back and makes his way behind me and wraps his arm around me. I grab his hand and interlace our fingers as I feel his chin rest on my head. "Love you, Max."

"Love you too, Jaycee."

The next morning at six o'clock my phone goes off and I smile. I missed Kid Rock waking me up with Bawitdaba.

Max chuckles. "What the fuck, Jaycee. Really?" he says, still laughing.

I'm laying on my stomach and he's almost completely on top of me as he reaches across me and grabs the phone to turn the alarm off.

"I love that song, Max. It's for his hoods of the world misunderstood, chicks with beepers and all his homies in the County in cell block six," I tell him with complete seriousness.

Max lets all his weight drop on top of me because he burst out laughing and I can't help but laugh too. He turns us so he's on his back and pulls me on top of him. I raise up on my elbows on his chest and look down at him and as he smiles, dimples on full display.

"Out of every song you could have possibly had as your alarm, I did not think that would be the one." he says while reaching up and smoothing my hair back from my face.

"Okay. Fair warning. Right now, I have three favorites I switch back and forth to wake me up," I tell him but don't say which.

He's still looking at me grinning and finally asks. "I give. Which three?"

"As you just heard, Kid Rock and tomorrow it will be Shinedown's 'Devour." I love that song."

Max shifts his head against the pillow and looks impressed. "Okay and the third?"

I smile because I know he'll get a kick out of it.

"Okay, well my third is Jerry Lee Lewis' 'Great Balls of Fire.' It always makes me smile," I tell him.

"Love, you make me smile." He chuckles.

All I can do is smile as he laughs. He looks over at the nightstand and grabs his phone to check the time; his face turns somber and I hear him sigh.

"I'm not liking this but we have to get ready for work. Jaycee, please, be careful today," he tells me through a grumble.

I know he's worried, but the threat is over and its time for us to move forward.

"Sugar, I'm fine now. We'll be fine. I don't want you to worry, okay?" I look down at him but he doesn't say anything, just stares back so I give him a slight nod, "I'm going to turn on the coffee maker."

I start to lift off him but he holds me tin place. "I know, love." He leans up and gives me a peck and swat on my ass. "I'll get in the shower while you do that."

He rolls out of bed and heads for the bathroom as I do the same, but head for my closet to grab my robe. It's not until I open the door that I remember I don't have one. Everything was ruined because of the fire. I take a deep breath and start looking through the rack of hanging clothes. A smile touches my lips as I pull out the old blue flannel Max was wearing our first day at the cabin and slip it on. That day, I thought I'd lost him, only to find out he loves me as much as I love him. I stand, still wrapping it around me, as I think back to taking it off of him. That was the first time we'd made love. I decide coffee can wait and walk into the bathroom.

The shower door is steamed up but I can still see his silhouette as I take off the shirt and drop it to the floor along with my gown and panties. When I open the door, he's standing with his face in the spray. I step in behind him and wrap my arms around his waist. He gives a little jolt but then puts his hands on mine and steps back towards me.

I lick and kiss his back and moving my hands down his abs. He drops his hands to his sides until I find him and start stroking. He lifts his hands and puts them on the shower wall as I continue to stroke him. He lets me do this for a few minutes but then he turns and pushes me up against the shower wall and starts kissing me. He moves his hand down to me and without hesitation enters me with two fingers. When he feels how wet I am, he grabs and lifts me up. I wrap my legs around his waist as our mouths crash together again. He holds me up with one arm as he uses his other to line himself up and enter me.

"Hold on, love. We're going fast and hard," he says against my ear.

I shiver at his words but grab hold. He doesn't waste any time taking us there. He stops kissing me and lowers his head to my breast, circling his tongue around my nipple, taking it between his teeth and tugging.

"Touch yourself, hurry," he commands, his voice husky.

I hold on with one hand and find myself with the other. In just a few seconds, we both come.

After we both calm our breathing, he drops me to my feet and then looks down at me. I can't help but feel a little embarrassed for my sneak attack, looking at him with worry in my eyes.

"I like the way you say good morning," he says

"I already said good morning. That was more of a 'have a nice day and I'm really going to miss you'." I whisper to him.

He gives me another kiss and pulls me into a hug. "Going to miss you too," he whispers back.

After our shower, still wrapped in my towel, I stand in front of the mirror as I throw on a little makeup and start to blow dry my hair. With the angle of the mirror, I'm able to watch Max get dressed behind me. He's wearing only his uniform pants and undershirt, sitting on the edge of the bed putting on his boots. I finally give up on what I'm doing because I'm so caught up in what he's doing. He's shaved off his goatee, but his hair is still longer than it probably should be. He looks up after tieing up the laces on his boots when he notices I've moved to stand in front of him.

"Umm, you look very military, Max."

"Good. Just the look I was going for." I reach out and run my hand along the smooth skin of his face.

"I like the goatee a lot but I like this too." He stands up and pulls me close.

"I can always gown the goatee out when I'm on leave," he tells me as he leans down and gives me a peck on the lips. "But for now, I need to head into work. You going to be okay?" He cups my face in his hands and pulls it up so he can see into my eyes. I smile back and bring my hands up and wrap them around his wrists.

"I'm going to be fine." After a long slow kiss, he steps back from me and smiles as he turns and grabs his uniform shirt, backpack and then walks to the nightstand to grab his keys and phone. He tucks them in his pocket and heads for the door. With his hand on the doorknob, he turns back to me and smiles.

"Love you, Jaycee." I blow him a kiss.

"Love you too, Max," I reply as he walks out A few moments later, I hear his car motor start up. I sit down on the bed feeling a little sad and lonely but I need to stay strong. I can feel a bit of panic setting in as I hear his car start down the drive and fade away. My eyes start to water but then the phone chimes with an incoming text. I smile as I read the text Max has just sent.

Love, I miss you already. Hope you have a wonderful day. Think about me. I will be thinking about you.

I take a deep breath and text him back with the promise that I will be thinking about him and I love him too. I can do this. I return to the bathroom to finish my hair and makeup and then get dressed in some comfortable jeans, my boots and work shirt. I throw on some hoop earrings, a few bangles and my favorite thumb ring and head into the kitchen for a quick cup of coffee.

CHAPTER EIGHT

While I'm sipping on my coffee, grandma walks into the kitchen in her robe and smiles at me. I can tell, she, like me, hoped for normal days to return.

"So, you excited to be going back?" she asks as she turns to the cupboards and pulls down a coffee mug and heads to the pot to pour herself a cup.

"I'm happy to be doing pretty much anything. Just thankful to the Lord I'm alive." I honestly reply.

"I hear you, sweetheart." she agrees as she sits at the table. "So normal hours?" I join her, knowing that I only have a couple of minutes, but I'll always make time for grandma.

"Yes, ma'am. I'm supposed to be there early today to get a quick refresher but it'll be eight am to four pm just like before." I have to admit I'm starting to feel excited. My shoulder sometimes feels stiff, but otherwise it's feeling pretty good. "I better get going or I'm going to be late on my first day back." I give her a kiss on her cheek before grabbing my keys from the key rack. I look back to her and I catch the worry in her eyes. The same look Max had. "Love you, Grandma, and I'm going to be okay."

"I know, sweetheart. But I worry. It's just what I do," she tells me with a sigh. "Before I forget, some of the girls and I are going to go see that new movie about the magician named Mike? Magic Mike. I think that's what it's called."

OH SHIT! "Um, Grandma, that movie isn't about a magician named Mike. It's about a guy whose name is Mike and he str..." and she cuts me off.

"Sweetheart have you seen the movie previews of his moves? He's magic alright." she tells me.

Oh shit, blah, blek and gag! "Ugh! Grandma. That's not cool. I'm outta here. No more sharing unless it's recipes, please!" I shudder, as I head for the door, her laugher following me.

Sorry, Channing Tatum, Grandma just ruined you for me, forever!

After starting my car, I notice it's been detailed. I'm guessing my dad probably made sure it was in working order. I get to see them all this weekend when we go to my Uncle Brock and Aunt Paige's to finally meet Callie. Butterflies tickle my stomach at the thought of meeting this precious little girl. I get the CD I want loaded, Billy Currington, That's How Country Boys Roll and I'm off pulling down the driveway for work.

CHAPTER NINE

I park in the back employee's lot of Dan's Grocer and head to the side door with my key card out. Before I swipe it, I take a deep breath and tell myself this is one of many steps I'm going to have to take in order to get my life back to a place I feel safe and normal again. I need to do this. I won't let Rocky take away my future happiness. I'm moving forward with Max and our families. Hopefully some day in the not too far future, we'll be starting our own life and family together.

I swipe the card and when I hear the click, I pull the door open and head in. I start down the hall to the break room that holds the employee lockers but I stop in my tracks when I get to the doorway. The scene that greets me has tears springing to my eyes and it takes me a moment to catch my breath. The entire room has been decorated with balloons and streamers; a *Welcome Back* banner hangs in the center of the room and standing beneath it is Nora Lee, Bernice and Kaytlin.

Their faces break out in grins when they see my reaction; each obviously pleased that their effort had the desired effect on me.

"Oh wow, you didn't have to do this for me." I open my arms as Bernice walks up and gives me a big hug.

"We know we didn't but we wanted cake." I laugh

as she pulls back from the hug and Kaytlin rushes over to take her place.

"It was early so we got donuts too. We'll do the cake around lunch time." Kaytlin says as she squeezes me a tightly and rocks us side to side. "Glad you're back. Nora Lee was driving us crazy."

Nora Lee making a scoffing sound. "I'm driving y'all crazy? You can't be serious. Ya'll drive me crazy. I'm surprised I haven't been locked away in the looneybin."

"Me too." Bernice mumbles.

"Maybe she escaped. We should call the state hospital. See if they're missing anyone. Give 'em a heads up to head she's over here and to come get her." Kaytlin adds with a giggle.

I can't help but laugh. I sure did miss this. Nora Lee pushes them to the side and comes forward but stops and points to Bernice and then Kaytlin.

"You two, y'all are going to make me cross over." We all start laughing as Nora Lee pulls me into a quick hug. "The others will be here at their normal time. We wanted to give you some quiet time to walk around the store and get reacquainted with the register." I nod as a thank you. "If you want to shadow for a while, go ahead. We have plenty of people so just take your time and get comfortable."

Kaytlin and Bernice grab my hands and we start walking through the store. They catch me up on work gossip and tell me about a few new cute male customers that have been coming in. We get to the front of the store where the registers are and they stand back and talk while I familiarize myself with the everything. After doing that for a few minutes, we walk back towards the deli and storage room. We spend some time walking through the aisles of products until we hear Nora Lee page us to the break room. When we get there, the morning shift has arrived and everyone takes turns welcoming me back and giving me hugs. It's about ten minutes before we open so I head toward the employee locker room to grab a few things when my phone dings. I pull it from my pocket and see a text message from Max.

You'll be great. Love you. He knows I'm stressing and even though we aren't together he's still making me feel safe and loved.

I love you too, I quickly text back and put my phone in my locker and head out front to checkout.

After watching and helping the others bag items for a while I decide to get back into the swing and go to my register and turn my welcome light on. After the fourth or fifth customer, it's like I was never away. There's a slow down after lunch so we all take a few moments for bathroom breaks and to organize our work stations. I'm leaning down to grab some bags from underneath my counter when I hear a man's voice, "You're new here, huh?"

I look up, embarrassed to be caught off guard and see a man who looks to be a little older than me standing on the other side of the counter holding a loaf of bread and a gallon of milk. He's smiling but there's something not quite right about it. I stand but take a few steps back and reposition myself with a couple of feet between myself and the counter. I look around to make sure I'm not alone; relieved when I spot Bernice and Kaytlin close and checking out customers. I take a deep breath and try to relax a little. If I've learned anything, it's to trust my instincts and something is off with this guy.

"Yes, something like that." I wait for him to set down the milk and bread so I can ring them up, but he just stands there looking at me, tilting his head as if assessing me. I don't know this guy but I'm guessing he's probably just a creep.

"Um, did you want to buy that?" I ask gesturing to the items he's holding.

"Sorry. Yes." He laughs and sets them on the counter.

I logon to my register and pick up the milk to scan it. "I'm Jedidiah, but my friends call me Jed. You can call me Jed."

I send him what I'm sure he knows is a fake smile. Creepy name for a creepy guy and I won't be calling him Jed or Jedidiah.

"Hi. Nice to meet you. I'm Jaycee." I replay as I scan the milk.

"I know who you are," he tells me.

I'm reaching for the bread when his words cause me to freeze. His eyes bore into mine as he watches me closely. Sweat starts to pop out on my brown and panic

98

slides down my back. He knows my name? Just as I'm about to run screaming from my station, he speaks again. "Your name tag, Jaycee." He points to the small plastic square pinned to my chest.

I laugh a little nervously and feel a bit embarrassed. "Oh, yeah." I scan the bread and load his things into bags. He hands me a twenty-dollar bill and I ring it up and give him his change and receipt. It almost drops to the ground when I try to avoid touching him but he catches it.

"Everything alright, Jaycee?" he asks as he tucks his change in his front pocket. His voice is laced with insincerity. It's almost taunting. What's his problem? The panic begins to rise again when I hear Bernice call out.

"You okay, Jaycee?"

I don't answer. I'm frozen. I don't know if I'm imagining things. I don't know if I should run. I watch almost in a daze as he walks off while still keeping his gaze trained on me. I feel like all the progress I've made was an illusion because here I am unable to breathe. The girls are by my side in an instant.

"Turn off her light. I'm taking her to the break room. That guy is such a fucking weirdo. We should have stepped up when we saw him here." Kaytlin says to Bernice. She flips off my light as she takes my other arm.

"I'll go with you." Bernice says and they lead me down the aisle. As we're walking, I start to come back to myself.

"Okay, so it's wasn't just me? He gave y'all the

99

creeps too?"

Bernice mock shudders. "You have no idea, Jaycee. Dude is as shit creepy as they come. He's like the Norman Bates meets Lawnmower man creepy. He must be new to the area because he just started coming in a couple of weeks ago. He walks up and down the aisles and hangs out near the registers like he's a spy or something and then when he checks out, he only buys maybe gum or a soda. Today was the most I've ever saw him buy or even say." Bernice tells me.

"Awesome. Lucky me," I say under my breath.

When we make it to the break room we all sit down. Nora Lee comes out of her office and starts over to us.

"What happened? Are y'all okay?" she asks, concern evident on her features.

We all shake our heads but Kaytlin answers her. "That super creepy guy went through her line and gave all of us the heebie jeebies. I think Jaycee was a bit more sensitive to his creepiness."

She comes over and sits down with us. "I've seen him in here. Boy, are you girls right. Do me a favor and keep an extra close eye on each other when he's in here. We all have the same feeling, but until he does something wrong, I can't ban him from the store. For now, just be extra vigilant, okay?" We all nod. "Okay, let's cut the cake and take turns letting everyone come back for some and then, Jaycee, you can take it home with you."

"I'll take a few pieces home for my grandma and

Max but y'all can keep the rest here." I tell her as she starts to stand. Bernice starts clapping and I grin when I see her finish with a fist pump. Okay, despite Norman Bates meets Lawnmower man, Jedidiah/Jed guy, I'm having a good day. I've missed everyone so much. I'm so thankful to the Lord to be back.

About fifteen minutes before I'm to clock out, I start getting my till and paperwork together to turn into Nora Lee. I walk into her office and she stands and takes the till and places it in the safe. She doesn't sit back down behind her desk but instead walks over to me.

"So, did you really feel okay up there?" she asks and I smile at her.

"Yes, sorry about freaking out over that customer. I'm okay. I'll do better." I promise and lower my eyes to my feet.

When I hear her whisper my name I look up and her expression is soft. "Jaycee, you did wonderful. I'm so proud of you. You're taking your control back. Not everyone can do that. Some give up. Some stay. Some leave too late, but we all leave with scars." Her voice becomes thick with emotion. "Don't let this defeat you. Keep fighting. The Norris', they gave me back my fight." she waves her hand for me to close the door and then points for me to sit in the chair. She stands beside her desk and leans against it as she starts to speak. "You, like me, have people in your life to fight for you. Fight with you. Jaycee, I'll fight for and with you." She takes a deep breath before she goes on.

101

"A few years ago I found myself in a situation where I was a victim but now I'm a survivor. If it weren't for the Norris', who were my next door neighbors, I'd probably be dead or close to it. They knew I was too scared to call the police when my boyfriend at the time was hitting me but they weren't. Every single time they heard a cry or crash they called 911 and the police would come and hall my ex off to jail. They'd come over, nurse me, tell me I was better than this life and deserved more. They offered me money to just run, or a room in their very own home so they could protect me. I'd always been too scared to leave. One night when things got really bad, my ex threw me out the door and I fell down on the driveway. I was bleeding and couldn't move. My ex had his arm raised and was about to hit me again when Mr. Norris came out with his shotgun. He shot it in the air and then pumped it, walked right up to us, put it an inch from my ex's face and dared him to touch me again without ever saying a word. I'd never seen Mr. Norris look like that. He was shaking. I could tell it was taking everything in him not to pull the trigger. Luckily, Mrs. Norris had called the police. Once we heard the sirens, he lowered the gun and walked calmly back into the house as Mrs. Norris pulled me off the ground and helped me into their home.

She cleaned me up as the police questioned me. That night they took my ex to jail and because of repeated arrests, the judge denied bond and a month later there was a short trial in which my ex pleaded guilty to all counts and is serving five years. He's been in four and will probably get out early for good behavior. Behind bars he suddenly became a model citizen and a righteous Christian." she sighs and goes to sit behind her desk as I listen to her in disbelief. This woman is tough as nails or so I thought. I can't imagine going through what she did and knowing that the man that hurt her is close to having his freedoms back. I feel myself hiccup with emotion.

"That night, Mrs. Norris told me about their only daughter, Christina, who got involved with an abusive man. They didn't know. She started using drugs to deal with the emotion and physical pain living with a man like that was doing to her, and she hid everything from them. They thought she'd just turned off onto the wrong path. Christina committed suicide about eight years ago but she left a letter confessing what was really going on and begging her parents' forgiveness. She just couldn't go on and didn't want to hurt or hurt them anymore. I can relate, Jaycee. Those thoughts crossed my mind too." I watch as her eyes water and she looks down at the papers on her desk. She clasps her hands together and then brings her eyes back to mine. "I was heading down the same path and I guess they sensed it. Told me they needed me to help with their store for just a little while and then they'd help me move on. Mr. Norris is the Dean of one of the Universities. This store belonged to Mrs. Norris' parents. When her father and then a few years later, her mother passed, they took it over but needed help. That was four years ago." I watch as she smiles.

"They kept me so busy. Always calling me, *me*, for help." She shakes her head and sighs again. "They knew my self-worth was gone and they gave it back to me. They knew if I were still and quiet, I'd reflect on the negative since that was all I'd known for so long, so they kept me busy with positive productive things. Seems like it was months before they left me alone. They wanted to give me good thoughts to have when I needed them." A few tears roll down her cheeks and she wipes them away. "They saved my life."

"I'm so sorry you went through all that." I whisper, shaking my head.

She smiles and stands and walks over to me. "I'm not." She pulls me by my hand to stand and looks me in the eye. "Not me. It made me strong. I found a new family. A strong, loving family that taught me wonderful things about others and myself. I found a side of me I never knew existed and you will too."

I get what she's saying. I take a deep breath and pull her close. "Thank you, Nora Lee." It goes without saying that it took a lot to share this with me. I'm so grateful. I walk out of her office and head to my locker. After grabbing all my things out, I find my keys from my purse and look at my phone. No messages. I swipe the screen and send Max a quick text letting him know I'm heading home. I wait a couple of minutes but when I don't get a reply I start for the employee back entrance. I glance over a Nora Lee's door and call out, "See you in the morning."

As I turn my back to push the door open I hear her yell back, "Don't be late, Jaycee!" I smile and push the door open as my phone chimes.

Couldn't wait another minute.

Huh? I stop and stare at my phone, trying to make sense of Max's reply. I slip it in my pocket and continue on towards the employee lot. When I look up and see Max leaning against my car with flowers in his hands, I smile and rush over to him and he opens his arms just in time to catch me. I press my lips to his and let him know how much I missed him and how glad I am to see him.

After a mini make-out session, we both get in our cars and he follows me back home. When we get inside, I go to the kitchen and find a vase for the flowers. I put them in water, and then make my way to the bedroom where Max has changed into some basketball shorts and a t-shirt. I cross to my dresser and pull out some of my Victoria's Secret pink yoga pants and an oversized off the shoulder sweatshirt. I'm changing when Max comes back out and sits down on the end of the bed and watches me. After I get changed and drop my dirty clothes into the hamper, I walk over to Max and straddle his lap and stare into his eyes and I finally release a breath I'd been holding since that creepy Jed customer came through my line...Even with everyone's reassurance until I made it back safely into Max's arms, I wouldn't be able to really relax.

"Well, we made it through the day." he says with a smile.

"Well there's was a moment I almost broke and called you to come to me." I admit and look down. "I got scared." I whisper, a little ashamed I'm not stronger.

"Scared? Why? What happened?" Max asks and I

feel his body tense as he goes on alert. Anger, fear and concern flash across his face so I quickly try to ease him.

"It was just me, sugar. A customer came through the line and I was paranoid or he was really creepy—" Max cuts me off before I can continue.

"What do you mean creepy?" he demands.

"Sugar, it was nothing. Kaytlin and Bernice told me that all think he's creepy. I thought it was just me and I started feeling panicked, unsure if I was ready to be out on my own but once I found out it wasn't just me, that this customer, Jed, he's just super creepy, I was okay." I say trying to reassure him.

I push him back on the bed and follow him down. "I sure did miss you, Max." I say and lean down and kiss him.

He runs his hand up my back and tugs my hair gently. I raise up and look down at him.

"But you're okay?" he asks searching my eyes, still not believing me.

"Yes, Max. I'm sorry. I didn't mean to worry you." I say and frown knowing I've upset him.

"Love, you didn't upset me. I want to know everything about your day. Every minute. Especially if something upset you." He pulls me back down and kisses me. After a moment he pulls back. "Listen, trust your instincts Love. Always. And if this Jed guy comes back in again and makes you feel uncomfortable, you tell me someone else to take care of him okay?" he tells me.

I nod but he's not satisfied. "Promise me, Jaycee. Promise me if this guy makes you uncomfortable you go to the back and make sure you tell someone." He stares into my eyes until I finally promise.

"I promise, Max."

He rolls us to where he's on top and I immediately let me legs falls apart as he rests his body between them. He starts kissing me again and I feel his hand go to my neck and he lifts my head higher to his so can deepen the kiss. Things are starting to get heated when we hear a knock on the door.

We pull apart and Max stands up and goes to the door as I fix my clothes. He looks back at me to make sure I'm ready and then opens the door. Grandma is standing there with her purse in her hand.

"Hey, kids. Sorry to bother y'all but the girls and I are heading out early to go to dinner and then to a movie. I know you two have had a long first day back so I just ordered y'all a pizza from Mr. G's, up the street. They said it should be here in about thirty minutes." she tells us as she reaches into her purse for her keys.

I give her a hug. "Thank you, Grandma."

She gives me a tight squeeze and backs up but reaches over and pats Max's shoulder. "Y'all get some rest tonight. I'll be home late so don't wait up." With that, she winks at me and walks off.

Ugh, gross. "Stop, Grandma. That's not right." I say to her departing back. She doesn't respond but I see her shaking with laughter.

Forget the saying 'dirty old men' because these 'church ladies' seem to be far worse. I look over at Max and he's grinning.

"Stop, Max. They're going to go see Magic Mike." I huff out and shake my head. With that he bursts out laughing.

"It's not that bad, Jaycee." He pulls me into a hug while still laughing.

"Really? Picture your mom and her friends going to see Channing Tatum take his clothes off and your mom being super excited about it," I say with my eyebrows up.

His body goes still and his laughing comes to an abrupt halt.

"Exactly." I say.

He looks down at me with a pained expression. "Not cool, Jaycee."

I raise my hand and point into the direction my grandma just went. "I know, Max."

We pick up a couple bottles of water and head out to the porch. I grab the throw blanket that's hanging off the straight back chair by the door and go sit on the porch swing. Max sets the bottles down and comes and sits next to me and I throw the blanket over both of us. He pushes it back and then puts one of his legs behind me and pulls me between his. He turns sideways so I'm back leaning against his chest. Then he grabs the blanket and repositions it to lay across me. With his other leg still on the ground he starts rocking us back and forth. I relax into him and think to myself this, this is the way I want to spend every evening for the rest of my life.

Max's arms wind around my waist and he pulls me closer and whispers in my ear, "I love you."

I put my hands and top of his and turn my face into his neck and kiss him. "I love you."

He puts his lips to forehead. "Will you go for a ride with me this weekend? I know it's been a little chilly but the flowers are blooming up in the hill country and I want to show you something."

I turn more into him and wrap my arm around his waist. "Of course I'll go."

"I know we're going to meet Callie on Saturday, so how about Sunday?"

I snuggle closer. "Sounds like it's going to be a perfect weekend," I tell him.

I raise my mouth to his and we start kissing. Once again, the kissing turns heavy but we're interrupted when a car start down the drive. We break apart and turn towards the driveway. The pizza guy is here but as the car door opens I correct myself. The pizza girl is here.

She bounces over and opens the velcro straps on the thermal pizza bag, pulling the box out. "Hey y'all!" She's practically jumping out of her own skin. "I can't believe it's y'all," she says as she tucks the thermal bag under her arm.

"What do you mean?" Max asks.

I stop from going in the house to grab my purse for some money and turn back to hear her explanation.

She hands the pizza up to Max and he takes it and places it on the table by the door. He starts to pull money from his shorts as she lets out a giggle. "Y'all are a local legend."

We both stop and stare at her but I finally find my way to stand by Max.

"Fell in love in high school only to be kept apart because of age and family. Years later when a madman strikes," I watch her eyes grow wide and she shudders but then calms back down. "Blue," she points to Max, "steps back in from, well, the blue," she rolls her eyes, "and saves the girl." She points to me. "Who is also his long-lost love."

Max and I both stare at her in shock. Holy Cow! Completely oblivious to the fact that she just rendered us speechless, she goes on.

"Mrs. McGinty tried to pay Mr. G for the pizza over the phone but he said to tell y'all it's on the house. He sends his best he's glad you're okay, Jaycee." She clasps her hands together, still grinning and staring at us.

Max flips through his money to hand her a tip but she puts her hand up to stop him. We both turn back to her as she continues to speak.

"Mr. G already gave me ten dollars for bringing the pizza though I would have done it for nothing." Her bubbly personality turns somber for a moment as she looks at me. "I'm really glad you're okay, Jaycee. We all are. You're a hero." She looks at her feet. "I know technically we're not supposed to know who you are but people talk." She takes a quick breath and then quickly goes on. "Last year, my junior year at UT, there was this guy. Something happened one night as I was walking to my car, it was bad and he left me hurt and with bruises." She looks at us with tears in her eyes, "I never told anyone. I was too embarrassed. I was a cheerleader. He was football player and very popular."

My heartbeat quickens and my pulse races with anger for this beautiful young girl who should never have experienced these things. I wait, knowing the feeling of needing to get it out—I want to give that to her.

She frowns in thought but then takes a breath and carries on. "Me and some of my friends, we were talking about what happened to you after you were kidnapped. It was a wake-up call realizing it could be one of us and we all started sharing stories. I'm not the only girl who has been hurt and he's not the only guy who hurt girls on our campus. Some of us decided to tell our parents and administrators. Along with our parents and admin, we went to our dean. He suspended the guys involved pending an investigation. Our dean also started classes on self-defense, bullying and domestic abuse and stepped up security on campus. The guys involved can't come back to school until they take those classes and anger management." She gives us a beaming smile. "So, y'all are local legend like I said. "Like Romeo and Juliet," she starts giggling again. "Only you live happily ever after of course."

She turns and starts walking back to her car when Max calls out to her. "Hey, What's your name?"

She looks back at us and to Max with a little blush on her cheeks. "Bella. Isabella Rollins."

"It was nice to meet you, Bella." Max tells her.

I break from Max and walk down the steps and over to her. I pull her into a hug and whisper in her ear. "I'm so glad you're okay, Bella."

"You too, Jaycee," she says softly and wraps her arms around my waist.

"Bella, any of the assholes give you any more problems, you tell someone. You come tell me if you have to." Max tells her.

"I will, Blue. Thank you."

She gets back in car as Max and I stand and watch her turn around and start down the drive.

She waves and yells out the window. "See y'all next time!"

I look over at Max with such admiration and love only to see him looking at me the same way. I place my hands against his chest and our gazes are full of the love we have for each other.

"Max, everyone has a story. I'm finding that once you share yours, others will share theirs." I give him a sad smile. "They're not all pretty, but I'm honored they share."

He pulls me to him and hugs me. He takes a deep,

soothing breath and releases me to pick up the pizza and open the door. We walk in and sit at the kitchen table and quietly eat. We're both deeply moved by Bella's words and story.

Later that night, as we lay in bed, I share Nora Lee's and Christina's story. We lay quietly until Max grabs my hand and pulls it to him, praying out loud to God.

He gives thanks and asks for continued love, blessings and protection for all of us. He names Christina, The Norris', Bella, Nora Lee and Scarlet along with Cole and Callie, me and our family's.

As I listen to his prayers for all of us, I fall deeper, never thinking I could love this man anymore than I do, only to find out how very wrong I was. My love for Max just reached a level I didn't know existed in myself until this very moment.

After we say Amen, I snuggle up to him and lay my head in the crook of his arm. I wrap my arm around his waist and pull my leg up across his legs. He turns into me enough to throw his arm around me and rest his chin against my head. We don't talk but I feel him take in a deep breath and then slowly release it as he pulls me closer to him. I'm not sure how long we lay like that because I fall asleep.

The feel of Max's hand lowering the strap on my gown and his tongue gliding over my neck and shoulder at a leisurely pace pulls me from my slumber. When his hand pushes me down, I roll to my back and he moves to lay on top of me. I pull my legs up and wrap them around his waist as my hands go to his head and I run my fingers through his hair. I lay still, taking in the feelings of love from him as he kisses up to my cheek and makes his way to my lips. He kisses me passionately and then raises up and drags my gown and panties off before pushes his boxers away and lies on his back.

"I want to watch you."

That's all the instruction I need and I climb on top and straddle him. I kiss a slow path from his neck to his chest and then make my way across and back up the other side until I reach his mouth. His hands go to my hips as he pulls me up. He starts to reach down but I stop him. My hands find him and stroke him several times before I position him at my opening. I raise back and slowly start to lower myself onto him. We're able to keep eye contact with the little moonlight shining through the window. Neither of us seem to be breathing. Once he's fully in me, I rest myself on him, watching his eyes become hooded and his lips part. I can feel mine doing the same. I begin to move slowly up and down as his fingers tighten on my hips. We are still silent. Our movements quiet and slow, not frantic. We keep this pace for what seems like hours but I begin to feel Max tense. I can tell he wants to take over but he's still letting me set the pace.

"Hurry, Jaycee," he whispers.

But I keep my pace.

After a few more minutes of my slow movements, he can't take it and sits up and wraps his arms around my waist and pulls me down on top of him hard. We both moan softly. He leans back against the headboard and bends his knees pulling me higher. He settles me on him and bends my knees so that they rest on the bed. One of his hands goes into my hair and tightens as he brings my mouth to his. Our tongues tangle as I rest my hands on his shoulders and start moving up and down and he matches my pace. His other hand travels down my back to my ass and squeezes as our lips stay together, never parting. Our moves are so slight but feel so strong.

"Love, lie back." He opens his legs and lowers me on my back and he comes down on top of me without leaving me. He pulls my legs up to wrap around his waist and then positions his hands beside my head.

I take my hands and move them to his and we interlock our fingers. He tightens his grip as he holds them down to the mattress and starts thrusting deep into me. He brings his mouth back to rest on mine, our heated breaths are mingling. When I can't take it anymore, I raise and bite his bottom lip, keeping his to me since I can't use my hands to pull his head to mine. He moans and his hips buck. I release his lip and lick where I've nipped him. I use my head to push his to the side and I kiss down his neck gently nipping him as I go. I know I can't leave marks in this area because they'll show in his uniform so I keep it light. He raises up just enough for me to reach his chest with my mouth. I lick and bite on his nipple and his hand tightens. I move my mouth to the top of his chest and start to gently suck and bite in the same spot. He tenses and releases one of my hands and moves his into my hair where he can cradle my head. He raises up to make it easier for me to get to him.

"You marking me, love?" he whispers.

The thought of it makes me flush with wetness and my legs tighten around him.

"Yes. You are mine." I whisper back and he pushes himself hard and deep into me.

I go back to gently sucking on the same spot on his chest for a few seconds before giving him one final kiss and lowering my head. Max relaxes his body and brings himself back down to me. His hand is still in my hair and he uses it to turn my head to the side and I feel his head lower. He kisses my neck and moves behind my ear and softly kisses me there. "My turn," he whispers and then returns to the area behind my ear.

As he sucks, bites and licks, I moan and start to struggle underneath him, needing more, needing him to hurry and give me more. "Shhh, love. You had your turn."

I groan as he tortures me into ecstasy keeping his slow pace. He nips and sucks in the same spot only stopping to run his tongue slowly along my collarbone. His hands find my breasts and he gently twists and pinches my nipple. His hips start moving more forcefully as he continues to suck on the now overly sensitive spot on my neck. Out of nowhere my orgasm hits me, slow and strong. He doesn't pick up his pace. He keeps moving slowly while torturing my nipple and sucking on my neck. It makes my orgasm last forever. I need to scream but instead I turn and bite down on his bicep and moan. I try to concentrate on not biting too hard but I know I must be close to drawing blood.

When I finally come down, I relax my mouth and kiss his arm, dropping my head back to the side.

It's long before he finally picks up speed and his thrusts become more urgent. Fisting his hand in my hair, he groans out his orgasm. We both lay there, him resting on top of me for a few seconds.

"Stay here," he tells me as he jumps out of bed and goes into the bathroom.

After he cleans up he walks back out and over to me with a washcloth. He pushes my knees apart and gently wipes himself from me. This gesture is more intimate than making love to him. It overwhelms me every time. He walks back into the bathroom and throws it into the hamper and then comes back and slides into bed and pulls me back to him.

"Sorry I bit your arm, but you kind of deserved it," I whisper.

His body shakes with silent laughter and he kisses the top of my head. We don't say anything else as we fall back to sleep.

The next morning, we get up and after sharing another shower we head into the kitchen for some coffee. Grandma is already sitting at the table drinking from her cup and flipping through a magazine.

"Morning, Grandma," I say as I lean down and give

her a peck on the cheek.

Max grabs his travel mug and starts fixing himself a cup for the road and pours a second cup for me. I smile at him gratefully as I grab the mug sit down.

"Good morning, kids," She has a mischievous grin on her face.

I know what she wants and I'm not biting but before I can warn Max he asks her, "So, how was your night out with the girls?"

A huge smile spreads across her face.

Great! I slump back in my chair. *Here we go.*

"It was really good, Blue. Thank *you* for asking." She glances over at me and back to him. "We had dinner at Texas Roadhouse and then went over to the Alamo Brewhouse for the movie." She fans herself with her hand and goes on, "Good Lord that man," she turns her head back to me "Jaycee, you have to see that movie. There was this one scene where he does this thing with his hips. Maybe Blue can learn..."

"Stop, Grandma! Recipes only!" I yell in panic. I jump up and put my hand out to stop her.

Max grabs his coffee and turns to exit the room almost running into the wall. In his haste, he turns back to leave the other way not realizing he's only a couple of feet from the doorway and runs smack into me as I'm trying to exit the room too. We get tangled up trying to get around each other when in desperation he finally just picks me up around the waist and carries me out of the room. He puts me down by the front door and his face is red with embarrassment

"Gotta think, Max," I tell him.

He just nods and gives me a kiss and walks out the door for work. I can't help but start giggling when I hear my Grandma laughing.

"That was great, Grandma. Nicely played. Love you." I pick up my purse and head out the door.

"Love you too, honey, and thanks," she calls back.

CHAPTER TEN

When Saturday comes around, it's time to finally meet Callie. I'm super excited and Max keeps grinning and shaking his head at me as he's getting dressed.

"What? Ugh, Max. Come on," I whine. "You don't get it. It's almost like having another little sister. Abigail and I are excited." I'm literally bouncing up and down on the bed waiting for him to be ready. "Hurry," I beg. "Let's go, let's go, let's go." I stand up and gesture for him to speed things up.

He puts up his hands in surrender, laughing. "Okay, love. Let's go."

I start for for the door but look back at him as he picks up his motorcycle key from the dresser drawer. "Um, Max?" I say with hesitation because I know he loves to ride on the weekend.

He absently calls over at me while sticking his wallet in his back pocket and then walking to the closet to grab our riding gear. "Yeah?"

"Well, I wanted to stop by the store and pick up a gift for Callie. Like a 'welcome to the family gift' or something." I smile warily at him.

"Okay, yeah. We should definitely do that." He leans down and gives me a quick peck on the lips as he hands me my jacket.

He starts to pull his jacket on but stops when he sees me still holding mine and staring at him.

"Problem?" he asks confused.

"I know you love to ride on the weekend but I want to get her a gift and well, it may not all fit on the bike." I try giving him my best full teeth smile. "I mean, like, you can ride and I'll drive..."

He drops his hands to his sides and cuts me off. "Jeez, love, how much you plan on buying for her? Please tell me we don't have to go to the mall." To my surprise, my smile widens but when he sees this, he looks concerned, afraid even.

Normally, I love shopping any given day of the week, for any reason, but this is different. Important. Special. The thought of picking out the perfect gift for this little girl, it has me emotional. I want it to be perfect. Something she'll love.

Max wraps me up in his arms. He holds me like this for a few minutes before speaking. "Jaycee, it won't matter what you get her, she'll love it and you."

I let out a breath and squeeze him around his waist. "I hope so." I lay my head against his chest. "I just want her to know she's loved. She may be too scared for us to hug her and show affection that way." I shrug my shoulders because I really don't know. "I want her to have something, you know, to hold, that's from me. Even if it's not me holding her she'll know it was from me and that I care. I can love her through whatever it is. Does that make sense?" I ask.

He runs his hand down my cheek while looking in my eyes. "Yes, it makes sense. I love you, Jaycee." He kisses me again, only this time it he doesn't hold back. The passion and the love we have for each other is conveyed through that kiss, warmth spreading through my body the longer we stay connected.

When we break apart, he puts his hand under my chin to bring my face to his. I stare in his eyes for a few moments. "What was that for?"

"I can't wait to put my ring on your finger and have my babies growing inside of you," he says, catching me off guard.

I stand in a daze thinking that didn't answer my question, my brain jumbled from his kiss. I'm having a hard time forming coherent thoughts, but his answer has sent little shivers of excitement running through me. I manage to take in that he's taken my jacket from me and walked back to the closet. He comes back jacketless, obviously having hung our jackets up and then drops his motorcycle key back down on his dresser. He picks up his car keys, takes another look around the room to make sure we're not forgetting anything and then reaches out for my hand. I take it and follow him, absently grabbing my purse from my dresser as we pass it on our way out the door. Good Lord, my man can kiss.

We stop by North Star Mall on the way over to see Callie and I think I go in every store looking for something.

Nothing is calling out to me and now I've hit a dead end of stores. I've literally walked from one end of the mall to the other, with no success. I turn to ask Max for help, but he's vanished. I start backtracking and halfway through I find him standing in front of an electronic store watching the sports channel that's playing on one of the biggest television screens I've ever seen. Dang, I lost him a long time ago and didn't even notice. I shake my head, giggling to myself as I wrap my hands around his waist.

His body rocks a little, startled. He looks dazed when he meets my eyes. He finally shakes it off and comes back to me and I can't help but giggle again.

"Hey, sorry. Did you get her something? You ready?" He looks around, I'm guessing for the closest exit. God, he sounds so hopeful that I can't help but frown through my laughs. He's out of his element. My answer is going to hurt me more than him.

"No, Max," I say and I watch as his face drops and gloom sets in. You'd swear I just kicked his dog, told him there was no Santa and stole his candy all at once. I give a sympathetic smile and pull him by his hand towards another store. He's literally dragging his feet like a little kid pouting. "Max, help me. What should we get her?"

"There were some HD televisions on sale over there." His face starts to light up again.

Okay, so maybe he can't help me.

"Max, we can't get her a television. She's only three years old," I scold him.

"Oh, yeah."

His stride slows and I turn to see what he's looking at. It's the mall entrance for a high performance auto store whose main entrance sits outside where they have bays to work on their high performance cars. He tries unsuccessfully to tug me that way.

"Max, why are we going there? You want to get her some tires?"

He looks back at me hopeful and I shake my head.

"Sugar bear, no tires or any car accessories," I laugh and he actually looks like he wants to cry so I give in. "How about you go in there," I point to the auto store. "And I'll go in a few more shops and keep looking."

We have to get going soon if we want to catch an early dinner at the seafood restaurant across from the mall. It's a hole in the wall with the best food, but the crowds get huge at dinner time. If you don't get there early you can sometimes wait an hour for a table. If I don't get done quick, we're going to be late. I give him a kiss and push him towards the auto store. "I'll be back in just a few minutes. Do you think you'll still be in there?"

He looks at me like I've lost my mind. "Yes, I will still be in there. Come get me when you're ready." He practically runs off.

I start back down the wide main hallway of the mall, glancing down at the stores tucked off to the sides but nothing. I'm about to give up when I see it. That's the place I'll find the perfect gift for her. The one I hope she'll remember and cherish the way I did.

My Grandpa had a sister who would often come for visits. My great aunt Ava and I called her 'my auntie Ava'. I remember my grandpa calling her, 'his Ava girl,' and that's where I got calling her 'my auntie Ava'. My grandma adored her too. They were always laughing when they were together like Abigail and I.

She looked like a movie star. The old-fashioned kind. Back during the *Gone With The Wind* days. She was stunning with black hair and blue eyes like my grandpa had. She always seemed to glow like she had her own personal sun rays. On one of her visits, she came into my room holding a package wrapped in brown paper and tied with a string. I was sitting on my bed coloring when she sat down next to me and set the package in front of me. I couldn't help the huge smile that spread across my face. Open it, Jaycee," and she sat back smiling, waiting and watching.

I tugged on the string that was in a bow and when I did, it released the string and the brown paper fell open. I looked down and there, in a stack, were the prettiest books I'd even seen. They seemed to be alive. I picked up the first one, Sleeping Beauty, then the next, Jack and Beanstalk, Cinderella, Snow White, The Princess and the Pea and Rapunzel. They were the most beautiful things I'd even seen. I remember flipping through the pages and being transfixed by the beauty of the princesses in those books.

Sleeping Beauty became my most favorite fairy tale over the years. I remember 'my auntie Ava' she said to me that day, "Jaycee, one day, when you need him, your prince, your knight in shining armor will come for you, too.

I walk into Barnes and Noble and head straight to the children's section. I find myself being drawn back to my favorite, Sleeping Beauty. I find the most beautiful hardback by Mahlon F. & K.Y. Craft. I flip through the pages and it has the most startling illustrations. The princess has long golden hair much like I imagine Callie's might be. The pages seem alive and are glowing almost like the one I had growing up. As I continue to glance through the book, I feel my throat closing and eyes start to burn with tears. I hope that one day she meets a prince, her knight in shining armor. I know in my heart he'll come for her when she needs him the most.

I turn and walk to the section with gift wrap paper and pick a simple brown and some string. After I pay for everything, I walk back through the mall to the auto store. All my sappy emotion comes forward when I see Max standing near some rims near the entrance of the store looking like he's in love with them. I continue to watch him, taking him in and emotion overwhelms me.

He's so beautiful and so brave. And he came for me, rescuing me right when I needed him. My thoughts consume me as I make my way over to him with my heart beating out of my chest. He notices me, turns and steps close. Seeing the look on my face he becomes concerned.

"Jaycee, what is it?" He asks.

I'm too embarrassed to share my thoughts. He'll think I'm being ridiculous so I don't answer him and look away.

He grabs my chin with his fingers and brings my face back to his.

"Tell me."

Meeting his gaze and seeing the sincerity there, I tell him. "You're my knight in shining armor. You are my prince."

He just stares down at me, not saying a word. Embarrassed, I wiggled out of his hold, but he grabs me from behind and pulls me flush against his body, bringing his mouth to my ear. "Jesus Christ, Jaycee. I love you. You're done, right?"

"Yes, I'm done," I snap out of my sappy emotional haze when he starts pulling me behind him towards the exit. "Max!" I tug on his hand, laughing.

"What?" he asks not looking back, still pulling me along.

"We didn't come in that way. The car is on the other side of the mall." I keep laughing as he changes directions.

"I hate fucking malls," he complains as he finally spots the right exit and heads towards it with me in tow.

When we finally get to the car, Max pulls his keys from his front pocket and hits the button on the remote to unlock the doors. He opens the car door and takes the bag with Callie's gift from my hand and places it in the back seat. When he turns back around, he slams his mouth down on mine. I freeze, knowing anyone can see us but when his tongue licks my bottom lip, I open and let him in. His hands grasp my hips and pull me to him as mine go into his hair. I forget the time, place, my name until I hear a familiar voice right behind me.

"Good God Almighty, get a room, you tramp!"

Max and I lift our heads apart and we both turn toward the voices. I smile when I see who it is.

Abigail and Nick. Well, well, well. Looks like baby sister and I need to have a talk.

CHAPTER ELEVEN

When I turn and see Abigail standing there with Nick, I know through my smile a look of surprise and question still hits my face when she smirks.

What the heck is this about? I use our sister telepathy to ask her, looking between the two.

Her eyes go to Nick and she grins, tilting her head. *Seriously? Look at him.*

I only caught a glimpse of Nick at the hospital and the day he was hiding in the trees at Rocky's cabin. The day Abigail was kidnapped and stabbed by Rocky. The day Rocky shot me and went over the cliff into the lake. The day Nick saved her life and Max saved mine. But now that I'm getting a good look at him, oh, My God, he's hot!

He's the same height as Max only buffer. He's wearing old faded jeans and a button down cowboy shirt with the sleeves rolled all the way up past his elbow. The snaps on the front of his shirt are undone just one too many. I lie. No, they're not. I should just walk over and rip the panels apart. Jesus, Lord, he has on cowboy boots and there's a big silver belt buckle showing through the tails of his shirt. He has shaggy dark blonde hair with light beard, whiskey colored eyes and an honest tan from the sun.

After looking Nick up and down, I glance at Abigail. *Oh yeah. He's hot.* I grin and lift my chin up towards Max. *Holy moly, sis. I got some stuff to tell you. You will not believe it.* I giggle and blush.

She looks over at Max and winks at him. *I can only imagine. The quiet ones, oh, yeah.* I hear her say to my mind and we both giggle. The guys are now standing glaring at us with their arm crossed over their chests.

They looked entertained, yet a little angry too.

"Love, how about you not check any other guys out while I'm standing right here next to you, or ever for that matter," Max says, raising one eyebrow. "Also feeling kind of violated and dirty from the looks y'all are giving." He reaches out for my hand, pulling me to him with a little yank in his pull.

Uh, oh!

I put my hands out to offer an explanation but before words can leave my mouth, Nick speaks up.

"Gotta say, doesn't feel good, being objectified. You girls looking at us like we're nothing more than a piece of meat, its offensive," he says with a completely straight face.

Abigail and I look at each other in disbelief. You can't look like they do and not be objectified.

Damn, our men are freaking hot, Abigail! They seem a bit sensitive, but hot. We gotta play this their way because, well, they're hot. Alpha males, their moods and hotness. I convey to her through my look and a tiny eye roll.

130

She shakes her head in defeat, in agreement with me.

I begin to apologize to Max and see he's trying not to laugh. I narrow my eyes and look at Nick and see he's doing the same.

Nick speaks up. "No, seriously. I have no problem being objectified. None at all." He raises his left arm and flexes his muscle. "I'll even let you touch," he winks at me.

"Oh, brother! Really, Nick, think much of yourself?" Abigail says with a laugh.

I look at his arm, the big muscles, and like I'm in a trance, I start to reach out to touch him. Max's arms circle my waist and he pulls me back to him.

"No. Don't even think about it," he growls and I drop my hand.

Shoot! What just happened? Nick has some voodoo power or something.

"Sorry, sugar. Not sure what just happened. That wasn't me," I say, then cough and clear my throat, looking down and concentrating on picking an invisible piece of lint from my shirt.

"Looked like you. As a matter of fact, it looked exactly like you," he growls.

"Well, looks can be deceiving because I assure you, that," I huff and blindly gesture towards Nick's direction. "*That,*" I add with more emphasis. "Was not me," I reply, while still not making eye contact and looking down at my jeans, smoothing out an invisible wrinkle. "He must have voodoo," I whisper faintly.

"Voodoo? Did you really just blame voodoo?" Max scoffs in disbelief.

"So, going to Uncle Brock and Aunt Paige's, Abigail?" I ask her and then start to whistle for no reason as I glance up at the sky, wincing from the brightness of the sun.

Max steps in closer behind me, wraps his arms around my waist and then turn us towards the car. I still can't see anything except black dots, but I can hear just fine.

Max leans down and whispers in my ear. "Whistle all you want, love, because later you'll be using that mouth for something else and rest assured, you just earned a spanking." He leans closer in and kisses my cheek before he turns us back around but keeps his arms around me.

I can't help it. I let out a whimper but finally my vision begins to return. Nick and Abigail are both standing still, looking back and forth between us.

"God, you're are the biggest dork, Jaycee," Abigail says.

"I know," I reply in defeat.

"So, y'all heading over to see Callie?" Max asks.

"Yes, we just stopped by here to get her a little something," Abigail replies, lifting the bag in her hand to show me.

When I see it's something from James Avery, we

share a smile. All southern girls love James Avery and if I guess right, she's got her a tiny charm bracelet with a few charms.

"And you?" she asks, finally shaking off the haze that is Max.

Max finally releases his grip so I can open the door and reach in and grab the bag. I lift it and show her the same way she showed me.

"I'm not even going to ask which one. I know which one because you read it to me a million times. I love it," she says with a smile.

"I can't wait and longer." I look at Max and smile. "Can we go?"

His eyes soften and he stands back and gestures for me to get in the car.

"Hey, have y'all had dinner? We going to Sea Island for an early dinner. Wanna come?" I ask Abigail and Nick.

"Okay, yeah, we'll meet you over there," Abigail replies.

We climb in the car as Nick wraps his arm around Abigail's waist and starts helping her as she walks. She's off the crutches but still wearing bandages that go around her mid-thigh. He helps her over to a huge Jeep Wrangler parked just a couple spots over from us and opens the door. He bends down and picks her up like a baby and then lifts her up and sets her the seat. My sister leans down and gives Nick a gentle kiss on the lips. I continue watching as she pulls her head slightly back and whispers something to him. He smiles and then leans back in for another kiss and then closes her door and walks around to the driver's side and jumps in.

I face forward in my seat and catch Max watching the scene as well. We share a smile as he starts the car. I know my sister, her bringing Nick around, for something like this, it's a big deal. Tonight we need to sit and talk. I can't wait to hear everything and share everything.

Max takes my hand and pulls it over to rest on his thigh and I lean my head back on the head rest, just watching him as he drives. I'm so in love with him. I hope that my sister is as happy as I am.

After a nice dinner at Sea Island we make our way to see Callie.

CHAPTER TWELVE

When we pull up in front of my Uncle Brock and Aunt Paige's house, I see most of the family's cars parked along the curb and in the driveway. I jump out of the car as Nick's jeep pulls in right behind us. I grab the gift from the backseat of Max's car and then it hits me. I haven't wrapped the book for Callie.

"Dang it! I need scissors and some space to work real quick."

"Hang on, love. I've got something," Max says, moving to the back of his car to open his trunk. I follow and wait beside him as he opens up his duffle bag and pulls out a pair of medical tape scissors, handing them to me.

"Thank you, Max." I lean in and give him a quick peck on his lips.

"Come on," Nick calls out me over and opens the back doors of his Jeep, allowing me to use the trunk space to work.

"Thanks, Nick," I say as I lay the roll of paper down and start unrolling it. After I cut it, Max hands me the book. Once I have the paper folded around the book, I look over at the string. Here's the tricky part. Luckily I have an extra pair of hands.

"Sugar bear, please hold this down," I say absently as I keep working.

Max holds the paper while I turn to grab the string. I measure and cut it then tie it around, securing the paper tight and then into a bow. I stare at the package and think back to 'My Auntie Ava' and take a deep breath.

This is when I notice Nick and Abigail laughing and Max glaring at them. What the heck happened? What did they do to my Max?

I start to say something to them but I stop when I hear Nick say, "Sugar bear?"

Fuckity fuck! This is all on me.

I give Max my sweetest, most innocent look. I even bat my eyes before I try to make excuse, "I wasn't thinking. Sorry," I tell him as I walk the short distance to him and wrap my hands around his neck and lean in for a kiss.

Max leans back in and kisses all sense out of me. I think I'm completely forgiven but when we break apart, he says against my lips. "Jaycee, your ass is going to be so pink from my hand tonight."

My body jerks and I look up at him and catch his smile. The promise behind his eyes sends a thrill of anticipation through me. I should misbehave more often.

He takes my hand as we wait for Abigail to finish working on her gift. She places the tiniest pouch into the tiniest gift bag and then folds and slips a tinier piece of tissue paper inside. When she's done, we grab our gift bags and head towards the door to meet the newest member of our family.

CHAPTER THIRTEEN

Abigail and I take the lead up the walk that leads to the front door. I push the button on the doorbell and stand back as it chimes. A shadow comes across the stained glass of the front door and then Jesse appears. He greets us holding the most beautiful little girl I've ever seen.

Her head is laying against Jesse's shoulder with her face almost completely buried in his neck. Her hair is a beautiful light blonde that hangs in ringlets down almost past the middle of her back. She has on the cutest white eyelet dress and is wearing brown cowboy boots with little gold stars on them. I can see she has a big yellow bow tied on top of her head. As cute as she looks, my breath leaves me when I finally get a small glimpse of her face.

"Princess Callie, I'd like you to meet your fairy godmothers, Abigail and Jaycee. Remember, the ones I told you about?" Jesse says, sharing his softer side people rarely see.

She nods but doesn't life her face from his neck.

"You're the most beautiful princess I've ever see, Callie," Abigail says. Although she's trying to help Callie relax, I can also tell she really means it.

Callie lifts her head but she's still looking down. I

can see she's smiling and deep dimples on her cheeks. She has a cute button nose, just like Aunt Paige described. She finally lifts her eyes up and looks right at me. Oh, my God, I inwardly gasp. Her eyes are the prettiest gray; they actually twinkle, yes twinkle, causing them to appear to have a silver star shining in them. They're breathtaking. She's breathtaking.

"Hi, Princess Callie," I smile at her and she smiles back. A second later her gaze shifts and she sees Max. Her smile gets bigger and she tilts her head back down and giggles. I know, kid, I know. I can only imagine he's flashed his dimples at and probably winked her.

Jesse finally lets us in. As we stand in the foyer, Nick closes the door as Jesse sets Callie down on her feet. She backs up against his leg and wraps her little arm around it as he places his hand gently on her head. It's obvious she's smitten with him but then that's Jesse's gift.

"Why don't we take them to the living room where everyone is and get them something to drink?" Jesse asks Callie and she smiles up at him.

"'Kay, Knuckle Jesse." She reaches for Abigail's hand and pulls her towards the kitchen, surprising us all.

"Knuckle Jesse?" Max repeats with a chuckle.

"Yeah, so what, sugar bear," Jesse says and follows Callie and Abigail.

"Touche," Max sighs in defeat knowing everyone knows my nickname for him.

"I want a nickname," Nick chimes in.

Abigail hears him too and yells back. "Let's play around with that later tonight." She pauses to blow him a kiss.

Nick reaches up, and grabs the invisible kiss and pretends to put it his front pants pocket.

"How about 'whipped' for a nickname?" Max asks, shaking his head.

"I was thinking more along the lines of Romeo," Nick shoots back.

"He dies, they die, double suicide," Max's retorts.

"Guess I'll let her pick," Nick says.

"Good idea," Max tells him.

Jake walks in from out of nowhere and right up to Max.

"Sugar Bear, Shakespeare, Romeo and Juliet?" Jake shakes his head, "Give it to me," he demands.

Max reaches around for his wallet and starts flipping through the pockets.

"What are you doing, sugar?" I ask and wrap my arm around his waist and lean into him. Max doesn't answer right away, a deep sigh releasing from him instead.

"My man card." He glares at Jake. After that conversation with Nick, I don't deserve to carry it anymore. Jake is here to confiscate it."

I can't help but break out in a fit of giggles, as Jake

walks off, pumping Max's "man card" in the air triumphantly.

"Don't worry, Max," I slide around to his front. "I'll help you earn your man card back later."

He laughs against my lips. "Thanks, Jaycee. You're the best."

"Um, Ansie Jaye?" a sweet tiny voice calls to me.

I pull back from Max and look down to see Callie standing there holding a bottle of water.

I squat down in front of her. "Yes, Princess Callie," I say and watch her smile, her dimples popping out.

She hands me the bottle of water using both her little hands.

"Um, my mommy said to give you this to you an' knuckle Max." She bends her head down while looking at Max from under her eyelashes.

When she says Mommy, I look up and see my Aunt Paige standing a few feet behind her with tears in her eyes. I can't help the tears that start to form in my eyes too. Before my emotions get out of hand, I take the bottle of water from her and stand back up. I hand it to Max and reach for Callie's little hand.

"Thank you, Callie. Now, let's go in the living room. I have a present for you." I laugh when I see her face light up and she tries to jump in excitement but her little boots are too heavy for to make it up high, making it look more like a skip.

Max catches my eye and he's grinning just as much as me.

"Cuteness overload is exactly what this one is," I say.

When Callie and I enter the living room, the whole family is gathered there. I smile at my grandma before turning back and watching Callie as she goes to my Uncle Brock and Aunt Paige. Max is talking with Jesse and Jake and I start towards him but when I hear a giggle I turn back as my Uncle Brock swings Callie up and situates her on his hip while she leans in and whispers in his ear.

Aunt Paige takes her into her arms then turns towards me. At this point, I realize I'm staring and the room has gone quiet. Everyone is watching Callie with her new mommy and daddy. The emotion is almost overwhelming. Before it turns to tears, Uncle Brock speaks up.

"Callie would like to know if her Auntie Jaycee and Abigail would like to see her room." he announces and winks at her, causing her to blush.

"I thought she'd never ask. Of course." Abigail says with excitement and she starts to stand, Nick quickly helps her, when she can't get up by herself.

She limping towards us when Callie wiggles down from Aunt Paige's arm and walks over to her.

"You have a owie?" She frowns up at Abigail.

"Yes, sweetheart, but it's much much better now,"

She smiles down at Callie, trying to reassure her.

Callie takes a deep breath and then leans in and kisses Abigail on the knee.

"Wow, Callie. Thank you. It's all better now," my sister gushes.

Callie's face lights up in a smile at Abigail and she takes her hand, pulling her over to me and grabbing mine too. She heads for the stairs and I sense my sister's hesitation. She doesn't want to disappoint Callie with her still being hurt, but she can't make it up the stairs without help.

Nick and Max appear beside us; Nick picking Abigail up with ease.

"Free rides up the stairs! Who else wants one?" Nick asks looking around but not down at Callie. "Anyone?"

Callie starts hop skipping again trying to get his attention and squeals. "Me!"

Nick feigns surprise and looks down at her, "Well, yes ma'am. Let me get your Aunt Abigail upstairs and I'll come back for you."

Callie stops and stands still as a statue with only her head moving as she watches Nick carry Abigail up the stairs and then set her down. Nick looks down over the banister at Callie. Her head is tilted so far back, it's a wonder she doesn't fall back.

"You ready?" he asks her as he descends the stairs.

When he reaches the last step, she takes off running

143

up to him and throws her hands straight up for him to pick her up. He reaches down and catches her, swinging her around so she's on his back. Callie giggles and squeals again in excitement.

Max and I stand and watch as Nick gives a laughing Callie a piggyback ride up the stairs. When he gets to the top, he sets her down and then looks back over the banister and down at me.

"Next?" he calls down to me.

I smile back up at him and start forward when Max grabs me and pulls me back to him.

"Dammit, Jaycee." he growls. "Stop that shit."

"Voodoo." I whisper.

Max leans down and puts his shoulder in my stomach and throws me over his shoulder. I can't help the girlie squeal that comes out of my mouth as he makes his way up the stairs with me hanging down. I grab on to his belt loops and steady myself; laughing as I bounce up and down.

When he sets me down on my feet in front of him, I come back to my senses to see Abigail laughing and Callie bent over giggling. Nick's chuckling along with others downstairs.

"Wow, Max. Thanks for the ride." I lean to kiss his cheek.

"Knuckle Max, I wanna ride like that." Callie pleads, reaching her arms up to Max.

"You got it, Princess Callie," he lifts her and throws her over his shoulder with much more gentleness than he did me, and turns and walks into her room with her giggling.

"Where to?" When she can't catch her breath long enough to answer, he gently swings around. "Callie?" He turns in circles. "Where's Callie?" he asks.

"I'm here!" she squeals, laughing.

"Where? Callie?" he repeats, playing along. "I don't see her anywhere." He looks back to us in mock confusion. "Do you see her?"

Before we can answer, Callie lifts up from his back and brushes the hair back that's fallen over her face. She's flushed red from laughing so hard and her little white teeth shine through her huge smile. She puts her little hands on Max's cheeks and pulls his face to hers.

She takes a deep breath and says breathlessly. "I'm right here, knuckle Max."

Max's smile goes soft along with his eyes. He's just fallen in love with this little girl.

At this moment, I decide I want at least a hundred of Max's babies. No, a million. However many God blesses us with, I will be happy but I want to start now. After watching him with Callie, my ovaries have jumped into action. I can practically hear them chanting "Max, Max, Max."

"Oh, there you are," he kisses her cheek and then

sets her down in the middle of her beautiful pink room.

She immediately starts dragging Abigail and I around her room. She points and shows us every little thing from her ballerina night light to a giant elephant that's sitting in the corner. That belonged to her brother, Cole. I remember seeing it sitting in a red wagon at his funeral. I think it's perfect that's it here. One day I'm sure my Aunt and Uncle will tell her about little Cole.

I come back to the present when she points to the elephant and tells us, "His name is Honk." She sits in the elephants' lap.

"Honk?" Max and Nick say at the same time.

"Of course, Honk." Abigail says.

"It makes perfect sense." I add.

"I don't get it." Max says slowly like he's missing something.

"Yeah, I'm lost." Nick adds.

Callie lifts up the elephant's trunk towards Max and Nick. "HONK!" she exclaims while flopping the trunk.

We all break down in laughter and Callie joins in. Cuteness overload, indeed.

When she's done, she gets up and walks over to her bed. She throws one of her tiny booted feet up on top and hefts herself up using her tiny arms. She rolls until she's in the middle of the covers and then turns and sits up and yawns. She does a slow blink and then gives a sloppy grin. She's had a lot excitement today and it's hitting her. About that time, Aunt Paige walks into the bedroom holding the gifts we brought for Callie.

"Like clockwork, seven o'clock every night, delirium sets in." She gives Callie a sweet smile. "You want to open your presents before you go to sleep, sweetheart?" My aunt asks as she sits down next to her. She sets the two gifts in front of her and Callie eyes briefly open wider in excitement as she lazily nods her head.

Abigail and I join them and watch as Aunt Paige scoots in closer to Callie and helps her pull the tissue paper from the James Avery bag bringing out the little pouch. My aunt turns the pouch upside down and the tiny charm bracelet falls into her palm. She smooths it out and we all lean in to see it. On the little silver chain hangs a tiara because Callie is a princess, the letter 'C' for Callie and 'M' as she's soon to be McGinty, and a cross just like Abigail's and I have on ours. That one binds the three of us. The last one I see is an angel. A little boy angel. Cole. Callie touches all the charms with her little fingers. She stops and stares at the boy angel and then gives the sweetest smile. It's like Cole himself just whispered something loving in her ear. My aunt puts her hand to her mouth and lets out a little sob and then leans in and hugs Abigail. We're all teary eyed when Callie reaches out her little wrist. She wants to wear her bracelet. Aunt Paige hands it to Abigail and she loops it around Callie's wrist and fastens the clasp. Callie looks down at Abigail's wrist and touches her bracelet and then looks over at me and down to my wrist and then reaches over and touches mine.

147

We all take a deep breath as Aunt Paige sets my gift in front of her.

"Open it, Callie." I whisper. She reaches down and tugs the tie until the bow comes undone. I watch as the string falls down and the paper falls apart.

Callie just stares at the cover. Her eyes scan the front, taking everything in. Finally, she reaches down and picks up the book. She struggles a little situating it in her lap because the book is almost as big as she is. When she pulls back the cover, the pages start flipping, landing on the one showing Sleeping Beauty laying down, asleep, wearing a shimmering gold gown with her beautiful golden blonde hair spread all over. The Prince is standing over her, about to kiss her. She reaches out and runs her fingers along the page.

"Pwetty," she whispers then lets out another huge yawn.

"Okay, honey. Let's get your jammies on and then you can tell everyone goodnight." Aunt Paige tells Callie as she picks up the book from her lap and sets it on the nightstand by her lamp.

I can't help but let out a soft laugh when Callie looks up at my aunt with a deep frown but then lets out another yawn and sways to the side.

"Your Aunt Jaycee can read the book to you after you get tucked in," Aunt Paige tells Callie as she gets up and walks over to the dresser and pulls out a lacy yellow gown. She grabs a beautiful brass hairbrush from the top and starts back over to the bed.

Abigail and I both laugh as Callie throws her hands up and then flops back on the bed. After a second, she rolls over on her tummy and I hear manic laughing from her as she buries her face in the bed. I'm not sure she can breathe but she's laughing so I guess she's okay.

I hear a deep laugh from the door and look up to see my Uncle Brock standing there smiling.

"It's time?" he asks.

"Oh, yeah." Aunt Paige laughs.

I hear another muffled manic giggle come from Callie, her face still buried in the covers and her little body shaking from her giggles. Abigail and I burst out laughing.

As Uncle Brock walks in the room, Abigail and I leave to wait in the loft. Nick and Max are sitting there talking so we make our way to them. Nick stands and helps Abigail over to the chaise and holds her as she sits down and then sits next to her.

When I sit next to Max, he drops his arm around my shoulder and pulls me to him and kisses my temple.

"She's a doll, Max." I say softly.

"Yeah," he says simply, kisses my head again. I relax against his chest and listen to Nick and him talk about cars until Aunt Paige pokes her head back out of the door and looks over to us.

"She ready and she's not going to last long." she says and ducks back into the room.

Nick helps Abigail walk back over to the room, and we peer into the room from the doorway. Uncle Brock leans down and gives Callie a kiss on her nose; she twitches it and rubs it. Again, she lets out a quick manic giggle but it quickly become another yawn.

Nick reaches her side and grabs her hand and starts giving it a formal shake. "It was nice to meet you, little lady." He leans down and kisses her hand. "It really was a pleasure, Callie. Until next time."

Max comes forward, bends down and gives her a kiss on her cheek and when he pulls back she smiles up at him and does a slow blink. "Sweet dreams, Callie." He and Nick leave the room.

Abigail and I resume our earlier positions, each on one side of the bed. I pick up the book and open it as Callie leans over to me and rests her head in my lap so she can see the pictures on the pages. Aunt Paige turns off the ceiling light, leaving only the glow from her beside lamp, before she and Uncle Brock leave the room. As I begin to read, I notice even Abigail is listening to me and looking at the pages.

"Once upon a time there lived a King and Queen whose fondest desire was to have a child...a year passed, then three yet they remained without child..." I look down because Callie's weight has become heavier. She's fallen asleep and has her little hands tucked under her cheek in a praying position. Abigail smiles as she looks down at Callie. I start to close the book and move Callie when my sister stops me.

"No. Read it all." she says.

I sit back and reopen the book and continue reading. When I finish, I look up and find our dad is leaning against Callie's door with the tender expression on his face.

"Perfect. I love you both."

"Love you too, Dad." We both say softly to his retreating back.

"Big old sap." My sister whispers.

"Like a declawed grizzly bear." I whisper back.

We softly giggle as I switch a sleeping Callie back over so her head is on her pillow and pull her covers up around her shoulders and tuck them in. I lean down and give her a kiss on her cheek and a smile flickers across her lips. I smile back and then move so Abigail can say goodnight.

"Sweet dreams, Callie." She leans down and kisses her other cheek.

I put the book back on the nightstand and reach over and turn off her little lamp before I stand up. Nick must have been watching for some signal that we were done because he walks into the room and picks Abigail up and cradles her.

"You done, darlin'?" He asks.

"Yes." Abigail smiles and yawns.

"Did that story make you sleepy, too, Abigail?"

"Yes, honeysuckle. It always has." Abigail says

through another yawn and then drops her head on Nick's shoulder.

"Honeysuckle?" Nick repeats while smiling sweetly.

"Yes. I just decided on your nickname. You're sweet and bright and beautiful and your love surrounds and protects me like branches from honeysuckle. I love you, my Honeysuckle."

"Well, let's get you home and in bed, fire." Nick says and turns to the stairs.

"Fire?" Abigail asks sleepily.

"Yes, Abigail. You are my Fire. I didn't know I was walking around cold until you came along and warmed me like fire. I love you, too," Nick says in almost a whisper but I hear him and Max must also because he pulls me close to him and hugs me.

Love? Wow, they are serious.

"Goodnight, Abigail." I call over to her. She raises her head and looks over at me.

"Night, Jaycee." she says before wrapping her hands tighter around Nick's neck.

"See y'all later." Nick calls back to Max and I as he's walking down the stairs.

"Night, Nick." I say.

"Yeah, later." Max calls out.

Max pulls me into a hug. I lay my head against his chest and feel the warmth of his skin and the thump of his heartbeat. My eyes start to droop closed too.

"You ready to head home?" Max asks me while rubbing his hands up and down my back.

"Yes, I am." I drop my chin against his chest and just stare at him. God, he's beautiful. My eyes travel across his features, his dark hair and dark chocolate eyes, his dimples and full lips, white teeth against his olive skin. Yes, he's beautiful and he's mine.

"What are you thinking, love?" He asks while brushing my hair back from my face. He gathers it all in a ponytail and then grips it tight with one hand and uses it to tilt my head back.

A moan leaves my lips and I close my eyes as my hands drop to his sides and I grip his shirt in my hands pulling him forward.

"I'm thinking that I hope our sons will look just like you." I open my eyes and look up into his and keep going. "And our daughters," I answer breathlessly.

His grip in my hair tightens and he pulls it back farther, giving me a little sting.

"You really thinking that?" he asks.

"Yes, I want to have a million of your babies and I hope they all look just like you." I answer gripping his shirt tighter.

"When do you want to start having my million babies, Jaycee?" he lowers his lips to mine. "Soon?" he asks before kissing me.

Once we break from our kiss I answer. "Yesterday. I want to start yesterday."

"Let's go, love." He pulls back but keeps a tight grip on my hand as we both walk back towards Callie's room and peek in.

She's sound asleep with her little ballerina nightlight giving just enough light to see her hair spread over her pillow just like in the book. Our own little sleeping beauty.

We make our way down the stairs and say our goodbyes to everyone. Max is holding me close with his arm draped over my shoulder as we walk to the car. After I sit and get my seatbelt on, Max closes my door and walks around the front of the car and gets in the driver's side. One of the best songs ever to exist comes across the car's speakers, Boz Scaggs', *Look What You've Done To Me*. Max turns it up and takes my hand and rests it against the top of his thigh as he drives. He softly begins singing along with song, making my heartbeat race. God, this man. I love him so much.

CHAPTER FOURTEEN

When we get home, we walk into our room and Max turns around and locks the door. I feel my breathing quicken as he stalks towards me like I'm his prey.

"I know we were going to play tonight but I just need to make love to you." He lifts the hem of my shirt and pulls it up and over my head and then drops it to the floor. "Jaycee, I need to kiss every inch of you, taste every part of you." He kisses my neck, his warm tongue is doing exactly what he said. Tasting me.

His mouth keeps moving, down my neck, across my cheek and where he gently bites my chin before traveling down to my throat and then back up to the other side of my neck. My hands are gripping onto the sides of his t-shirt, holding on so I don't fall. Max slides his hand around my waist and pulls me tight against him and I can feel him through his jeans, pushing against my stomach, he's already hard. He keeps me there, against him, still, while caressing my neck and shoulder with his tongue. I can't stay silent, I release small pants and cries. His warm hands move up my back and unclasp my bra. He steps back and brings it down my arms. Only then do I release his shirt to let my bra fall to the ground. His eyes and hands travel to my breast and my nipples harden. He lifts them with his palms and pinches my nipples with his fingers.

My hands reach up as I run my fingers through his hair and pull his head down to them. He takes turns drawing each one in his mouth, sucking and biting gently. I'm already on the verge of coming. I whimper when Max pulls back and reaches down for the button on my jeans. When he gets them undone, he lowers the zipper. He runs his finger across the top of my purple lacy boy shorts but then lets his hand drop and he takes another step back.

My breathing gets heavy as I kick off my flip flops, slip my thumbs into the sides of my jeans and push them down over my hips. He comes forward and surprises me when he drops to his knees and puts his hands to the waist of my jeans and continues lowering them. Once he gets them to my feet, I lift one at a time while holding on to his shoulders and he tosses them to the side. He runs his hands up the backs of my legs, pulling me to him. I fall into him as he brings his mouth down on my stomach. I put my hands on his head and hold him close and he places hot wet kisses across my skin. When he stops and looks up at me with such love, my eyes tear up but what he says next has them dropping from my eyes.

"My babies are going to be in here." He says, placing more kisses on my belly.

Not being able to take much more and wanting and needing to feel him on me, in me I begin to beg. "Please, Max. I need you." I say through thick emotion.

He puts his fingers into the sides of my boy shorts and pulls them down and off. He tosses them aside, not caring where they land. Before I can register anything else, his mouth is on me. I whimper and grab on to his head, holding him there, pulling him in, needing more.

"Open." he growls and I widen my stance.

He continues to taste me and when I'm almost there I feel one, then two fingers start thrusting in and out of me and that's it, I explode. I scream out his name and dig my nails into his scalp as I ride one of the strongest orgasms I've ever had.

I don't even notice that he's carried me to the bed and laid me out for him. He pulls off his boots and then reaches behind his neck and pulls off his shirt. Only then does it register that he was still dressed and I was completely naked this entire time. I let out a low moan because that's a big turn on. What gets me whimpering in need again is when he undoes his belt buckle all the while keeping his eyes trained on me. My breathing becomes erratic as he unsnaps his jeans and lowers his zipper and then his boxers. My mouth waters when I see him spring free.

"Fuck. Come here." he groans, his voice hoarse.

I make my way over to him as he kicks off his jeans. I sit on the edge of the bed as he comes and stands in front of me, all the while pumping himself up and down.

"You want a taste of me, too?" he asks as he runs his fingers tenderly down my cheek.

"Please."

"Then, open."

I obey as he places himself against my lips with one hand and then grabs a handful of my hair with the other. When I reach out with my tongue and taste him, he moans likes he's in pain. I do it again and again, licking him up and down and giving kisses to his tip. His hand in my hair tightens, bringing me to a halt.

"Enough. Open." he growls.

I open and he starts thrusting in and out as his hand holds my head exactly where he wants it. I reach around and dig my nails in his sides and his thrusts become deeper causing me to gag. For some reason, that seems to turn both of us on. He grabs my chin with one hand and adjusts my head where he wants it. Our gazes stay locked, our connection never wavering until he finally starts to slow.

"Stop. Don't want to come in your mouth." He pulls back completely from my mouth.

He grabs me around my waist with one hand as the other goes to the bed. He lifts us and scoots us back so we're laying horizontal across the end of the bed. He wastes no time, when my legs fall apart for him, he comes down and enters me in one long hard thrust and immediately starts moving. He brings his mouth down on mine and his thrusts come almost frantic. The only sounds are our moans as he reaches down and pulls my knees up one at a time to wrap around him. I bring my hands to his back and start digging my nails in. He starts pumping faster. Finally, he breaks our kiss.

"Get there, Jaycee." he orders. "I'm there."

He raises up and sits back but keeps slamming into me. He looks down, watching our connection. I lower my hand down my stomach, across my belly button until I find the spot and start circling with my fingers. I can already feel the tightness and spasms start so I raise my hips up to meet his. He brings one of his hand to his mouth, licks his fingers and then pinches my nipple. That's it. My world explodes. I can hear myself screaming at Max to give me more and to never stop but my own voice sounds faint. My body drops in exhaustion. My limbs slide from Max, as my legs fall back to the mattress and my arms drop to my sides. I think I actually fall asleep for a few seconds but then the feeling starts to come back as Max drops down on me and starts moving faster. I can't believe it when another orgasm hits at the same time Max finds his. We both groan and just lay there, trying to breathe. Max moves from me so I reach up and pull him back down.

"Don't want to hurt you," he explains, kissing the side of my head.

Reluctantly, I let him up but lay in the exact same position and don't even move when he comes back with a warm cloth and cleans me. Once he's done, I turn on my side and snuggle into myself. Moments later, the lights go out in the room and the covers are tugged back. Strong arms lift and lay me on top of the cool sheets. Max climbs in behind me and pulls the covers over both of us.

I have just energy to tell him, "I love you forever and a day, Max."

He turns into me and drapes his arm across my waist and pulls me back against him.

"Love you too, Jaycee, forever and a day," he says against my ear and then kisses it and settles back down behind me.

CHAPTER FIFTEEN

The next morning, Max and I sit and enjoy a light breakfast and coffee with my Grandma before getting ready for the ride Max asked me to go on with him. My grandma is heading off to church and doesn't even ask about us joining her like she usually does. We enjoy going to church with her but some Sundays we miss. I go to the Wednesday night service if Max is working and sometimes if he's not, he'll go with me. One thing, regardless of whether we attend weekly services, we say grace together before each meal we share and every night before bed. I guess Grandma just figures we have plans so she didn't ask.

Like most mornings, our routine is to shower together. Once we're out, we start getting dressed. Max is standing in front of his chest of drawers wearing a pair of jeans still open with his black leather belt hanging loose, his motorcycle boots and a blue button down shirt that he hasn't buttoned yet. I'm totally distracted from doing my makeup as I watch in the mirror as he rolls up the sleeves of his shirt and then puts his watch on. His phone chimes alerting him of a text and he picks it up to read it. Sweat breaks out on his forehead and he starts to pale as he stares at his phone.

What in the heck? I start to ask him what's wrong,

but he cuts me before I can.

"I'll be right back," he says and fastens his jeans and buckles his belt in a rush; buttoning his shirt as he walks towards the door. "You're almost ready, right?"

"Sugar bear, are you okay?" I start towards him.

"I'm fine." he snaps. "Why?" His phone chimes again and after looking at the screen mutters, "Asshole."

"Max, really, are you okay?" I ask, beginning to worry. "We don't have to go on the ride if you don't feel well. Is something is going on?"

His phone chimes again and again and again, he fumbles with it but then it begins to vibrate.

"Jesus fucking Christ," he barks. "No, just stay here. I'll be right back."

As he reaches for the door, his phone in his hands sets off with another string of buzzes. He fumbles with it again, only to finally stick the phone in his back pocket, and walk out of our room. I can still hear it buzzing even after he closes the door. Between hearing his boot stomps through the house, I can hear buzzing and him cussing.

What the hell? Stay here, my ass. I open the door and follow him just in time to hear the front screen door open and him shout out.

"Really, assholes!"

As I rush through the kitchen and into the living room towards the front screen door, I can hear men laughing. Not just any men, my brothers. I should have known they were the behind this. Taking a deep breath to calm myself, I push open the screen door and walk out on the front porch with my hands on my hips ready to give them hell. I stop when I see them all freeze. Max's back is to me and it straightens up but he doesn't turn around.

"Hey brat," Jesse calls out along with other greetings from my brothers.

"Hey, sissy," Jake says to me and starts over to me. I narrow my eyes on him as he gets closer and closer until he's only a couple of feet in front of me.

What the hell are these bull asses up to now?

"Max!" I yell in Jake's face which causes him to grin and chuckle.

"Yeah, love?" He steps around Jake and puts his arm around my shoulder.

I can feel him shaking.

What the hell did they do to him? Nash and Chase step away from his bike. Max takes a deep breath and nods at Jake. With that, Jake leans down and gives me kiss on the cheek. Almost all my anger leaves as I smile up at the biggest of my big brothers. He shakes Max's hand and walks off not saying another word as he jumps in the driver's seat of his truck and waits for the others. Jesse walks up next and does the same. Then Nash, then Chase. They close their doors and the truck starts up and makes it way down the driveway. I turn to Max to ask what the hell is going on but before the words are out of my mouth he stops me.

"You ready?" Max asks, eyes still on the driveway.

"Max, what in the world was all that?" I ask his profile.

"What? What was what?" he asks, still not making eye contact.

"We really pretending that never happened?" I ask as I point to the truck that's almost out of view.

"It's probably best." He grabs my hand and leads me back to our bedroom.

He doesn't say anything else as he walks to the closet and grabs our jackets. He lays mine on the bed and puts his on. He pulls his gloves from his pocket and starts for the door. Still not making eye contact, he gives me a peck on the lips and walks out of the room.

Well, shit. He's serious. We're going to pretend that never happened.

In the bathroom, I make quick work of finishing my makeup. I throw on some jewelry and then sit on the bed and pull on my boots. I grab my jacket and slip it on and then tuck my driver's license and debit card in my back pocket along with my favorite MAC lip gloss, Mimmy. I won't need anything else today. I make my way through the house and when I get to the front door and look out, Max is throwing his leg over his bike, straddling it. He starts it up and then slips on his helmet, and gloves. When I get to his side, he pulls me forward by my hips and then grabs my helmet and secures it on my head. After he get it secured, our eyes catch each other briefly and he gives me soft smile as he guides me to hop on the back. Once on, I scoot forward and wrap my arms around him. We start making our way out of the drive and I glance back at the house to see my grandma standing by the screen door, smiling sweetly. As we pull out, she gives me a little wave. I smile, wave back and then wrap my arms around Max.

Max makes his way through the back roads till he hits Interstate 10. I hold on tighter enjoying the feel of the open air as he picks up speed. I lean my chin against his shoulder and watch as the scenery flies by. I love Texas, the rolling hills, seas of blue that magically transform into fields of blue bonnets as you get closer, Longhorns cattle standing looking majestic in their pastures. Then there are those fields that hold nothing more than a single, old live oak tree whose branches seem alive, with their brilliant twists and turns, they are enchanting. God lives here.

Max turns off on an exit marked, Comfort. It's a quaint little town with shops along its main street. I think we're going to stop for lunch but he keeps going right through the middle of town. A couple more miles down he turns off onto a farm road. I can see beautiful old homes sitting at the back of large lawns. As he rounds another turn, I gasp when I see an old metal train bridge that's painted red with the Guadalupe River flowing beneath it. It's breathtaking. A few more miles down, the bike begins to slow. Max pulls us to the side of the road in front of a beautiful field of blue bonnets mixed with a sprinkling of Indian Paintbrushes and comes to a stop. He turns off the engine and I sit taking it all in.

Neither of us move from the bike for a few moments. We sit quietly looking around at the beauty. I startle when I see something run across the street, causing Max to laugh.

"Roadrunner. Crazy looking little bastards." He shakes his head.

I can't help but laugh at his description, because he's right. He taps my leg so I hop off the bike and he follows. I pull off my helmet and set it on the seat and stretch a little while running my fingers through my windblown hair thinking next time I need to braid it.

"This is amazing, Max but what are we doing here?" I ask as he tugs off his helmet off and sets it next to mine.

While waiting for him to answer, I turn back and stare at the field. The beauty of bluebonnets across an open field never gets old. I sense Max moving behind me and then he stills.

"Jaycee." Max calls me softly.

I look over at my shoulder and I gasp when I see he's down on one knee holding a small black box. I slowly turn around to face him with my mouth hanging open. He coughs and clears his throat and then rubs his hand not holding the box against his jeans before he takes a deep breath and then looks right in my eyes.

"Jaycee Lillian McGinty, will you marry me?" He opens the box and lifts it to me.

My nose starts to burn and my eyes water as I look

down at the most beautiful antique ring. It's a silver band holding a princess cut sapphire surrounded by tiny diamonds.

I can't speak so I just nod. He jumps up and hugs me, lifting me until my feet leave the ground. I can do nothing more that wrap my arms around his neck and hold on tight.

"Really?" he whispers as he drops me back to the ground.

"Yes, of course I'll marry you, Max." I whisper back, lifting up on my tiptoes to kiss him.

He releases me and then pulls the ring from the box as I hold my left hand out for him. "This one?" He asks as he starts pushing the ring up my ring finger.

"Doesn't matter which, but officially, yes," I tell him with a laugh. After he pushes it on, he lifts my hand and looks at it for a few moments before he kisses it.

"It's perfect, Max. I love it," I tell him.

"When I saw it I knew I knew it was the one. I had to get it sized and the jeweler closed before I could get there yesterday so this almost didn't happen today" he says

"Did this have something to do with my brothers showing up today?" I ask.

"Yeah I told Jake and Jesse about it last night, Jake offered to pick it up for me and drop it off." He shakes his head. "Jesse sent out a damn group text this morning, to everyone, in your family, reminding them today was the day. Everyone knows, we've been keeping it a secret from you." He presses his lips to mine in a slow, leisurely kiss. "I have about a hundred texts on my phone ranging from threats to well wishes. I may have received a few pictures warning me of what would come if I messed this up or hurt you."

"Oh, my God, Max." A hysterical laugh escapes my mouth. "I'm so sorry. I think you may find I'm more trouble than I worth." I say, grinning.

His face turns serious. "Never, love."

After he breaks our kiss, he turns me back to the field of bluebonnets. I can't help but think how beautiful his heart is to find the perfect spot to propose. Giving me this beautiful memory. That is until he points to a hill in the field of bonnets and then proceeds to blow my mind and fill my heart even more than I ever thought.

"There." he continues to point at the hill.

"There, what?" I turn and look.

"There's where I'm going to build our house." he says and I slowly turn back to him. My eyes flicker between him and the field as he goes on. "Your dad came out and took a look at the property. He said it would be a good site to build on so when he gave me the okay, I bought it. It's yours. It's ours." he says like it's no big deal.

"Maxwell 'Blue' Bradshaw, how did I get so blessed? I love you." I whisper, my voice tight with tears.

I lean up to kiss him and when it becomes heavy, he

breaks away, his eyes scanning the area. Before I realize what he's up to, he pulls me into the cover of some trees.

After making quick work of my boots, jeans and panties, he tugs his jeans and boxers down enough to set himself free.

"Put your hands on the tree trunk." he commands, as he runs his fingers up and down me to get me ready; when he sees I'm already there, he grabs my hips and lifts me till I'm straining on my tiptoes. We share a moan as he slowly enters me and once he's fully seated in me, he wraps one arm around my waist and puts his other against the tree. He takes me like this, deep and hard, for several strokes but then turns and sits pulling me down on top of him. Now, I take him until we both explode. I lay my head on his shoulder and try to slow my breathing down.

"Well, it's officially ours now that we christened it." Max says and I start giggle as he chuckles.

We walk around the property for a while but then make our way back into town. We see a local restaurant proclaiming to have the worst barbecue in Texas. So, naturally we stop there for dinner before heading back into town, excited for what our bright future has in store for us.

CHAPTER SIXTEEN

Being lost in my own thoughts I don't notice we're not heading back home. Max keeps going back through San Antonio and exits on the outskirts of downtown. He takes the West Avenue exit and I know where he's going, Jacala's. Yay! When we pull into the small parking lot I breathe in the smells wafting out through their patio. My stomach felt full until that moment. Now all I have on my mind is enchiladas and puffy tacos. We make our way in the side entrance and Max pulls me into the back patio dining area and the entire family is gathered there. When we walk in, I smile and hold my hand up showing off my ring. With that, everyone starts clapping, followed by whoops and cheers being shouted out.

Chairs scrape the concrete as everyone comes forward offering congratulations, hugs and kisses. My sister hands me a bag and then hands one to Max.

"Let's get you changed." she says and starts pulling me to the ladies' room while pointing Max towards the men's room.

I feel a tug on my pants and a little voice call out to me. "An'sie Jayc, look!" Callie all but squeals.

I look down at Callie and she has a big black and white polka dot bow in her hair. She's jumping up and down, her little legs turn into skipping, to get my attention. She's wearing a blue jean skirt with tiny black cowboy boots. She's pointing to her shirt so I look. It's black, and on the front, spelled out in silver glitter is 'Blue and Jaycee' surrounded by a heart with an arrow pointing out the sides.

I reach down and pick her up, smiling. "Where did you get this, Princess Callie?" I ask and then give her a kiss on the cheek.

"An'sie Ab," she stops and her little eyebrows draw together in concentration, "b'gail." She takes a deep breath, frustrated with trying to pronounce my sister's name and decides pointing is easier as she lift her finger at Abigail.

"Remember what I told you?" my sister asks Callie, "You can call me Auntie Abby." She pulls Callie from me and sets her on her hip.

Callie smiles and then gives Abigail a kiss on the cheek, but then surprises me into a laugh when she blows a raspberry on my sister's cheek. Abigail wipes her cheek off as she turns to Callie laughing. About then, Nick walks up.

"Nice one, Callie." and Nick reaches for Callie. She goes willingly to him and he lifts her till she's sitting on his shoulders. "Hurry up. I'm hungry plus I can't wait to see Max's reaction to what's in the bag." With that, he leaves with Callie on his shoulders. After ducking a few ceiling fans, he leans forward and Chase steps up and takes her.

"I'm going to kick his butt for teaching her that. All day she's been giving me raspberries." She giggles and pulls us down the hall to the restrooms. "Hurry up, Max!" She calls back to him.

"Fuck me." he mutters after glancing in the bag before he disappears into the men's room.

When we finally get in the restroom, Abigail pulls me into a hug. "I'm so happy for you, sissy." When we separate, she pulls a t-shirt from the bag and hands it to me. "Hurry and change. I'm hungry too and I need some food in my body to absorb the margarita I had before you got here."

"Just one?" I ask while I unfold the shirt. I start laughing when I read it. No way is Max going to change if his is anything like mine.

"Okay, maybe two. You guys took forever to get here." She starts tugging at the hem of my shirt, trying to pull it off.

"Two?" I ask while slapping away her hands. I pull off my shirt and then slide the other one on.

"Yes, two. I haven't licked the salt from the rim of the second one yet and barely had a sip of three." she adds while busting into a fit of giggles when I turn to her. "You look adorable. Blue, probably not so much." She grabs my old shirt and stuffs it back in the bag. She takes my hand and pulls me out of the bathroom and back down the hall towards our table.

I already hear it. Hysterical laughter.

When I turn the corner, I can't help but start

laughing too. My poor Max.

There stands Max, wearing a black t-shirt with two cats embracing and it reads, 'together purr-ever' and on the back 'she said yes'.

He starts walking to me but stops when Jake walks up and hands him a beer. He lifts the bottle to his lips and downs half the bottle in one pull. He narrows his eyes on Abigail who's now close to passing out from laughter and then walks over to me.

"I used to like her." he says while wrapping his arm around my shoulder. "Not so much now."

"Max, sugar, I'm sorry but you do look adorable." I wrap my arms around his waist and smile up at him.

Nick hands Max another beer and me a margarita. "Did what I could. Count your blessings. She wanted it in pink." he informs us before continuing on his way.

Max steps back and looks down at my shirt and starts laughing. Mine has two owls with huge hearts as eyes and it reads, "hoo said yes?' and on the back, 'I said yes'.

We're both laughing when Callie walks up and raises her arms to Max. He sets his beer down on the table and scoops her into his arms. While the three of us are looking at each others' shirts, my sister and Violet aim their camera phones at us. We turn towards them and smile. While waiting for them to take the picture, I glance behind them and see a man with a full beard and long hair, wearing a pair of aviators. He's standing at the bar, watching us. I absently note something familiar about his stance; but get distracted when Callie squeals "cheese" for the camera.

But then it clicks. My world stops and my glass falls from my hand and shatters on the floor.

CHAPTER SEVENTEEN

"Jaycee?" Max calls to me as he pulls Callie and I from the broken glass.

I whip my head back towards the bar but I see no one. My eyes dart around while I try to process everything in my head. No one else is reacting. They're just standing around talking and laughing. They would have noticed, right? I take a calming breath as I take one more look around. Nothing. I'm just seeing things.

"Jaycee, love?" Max hands Callie to my Uncle Brock and pulls me to sit down at a chair by our table, squatting down in front of me.

I laugh nervously. "Sorry, sugar bear." He narrows his eyes on me before deciding to let this one slide.

"You okay?" he asks while looking over his shoulder at two bus boys that come in and start cleaning up the broken glass.

"I'm fine." I smile. "Sorry about that." I call out to the boys cleaning up the broken glass. They just smile and give a polite wave and go back to sweeping up my mess.

"I want some puffy tacos is all, Max.

"Well you didn't have to start breaking things to get

them." He laughs while pulling me close for a hug. "Let's get you some tacos before you start tearing this place apart."

"Good idea." I say while he takes his seat next to me and picks up the menu.

During dinner, Callie laughs and cuts up with everyone. I remember being worried about her adjusting, everyone was. If anything, she's come completely out of her shell and blossomed into a beautiful, happy little girl enjoying life. She's an absolute joy and a little bit of a firecracker. Whoever she was with before us loved her too. I don't know her entire story, none of us do, but this little princess did not come from abuse.

I glance over at Max and he's watching me watch her. I smile when our eyes meet.

"I'm not sure what I was so worried about." I say absently. "It's almost like there was never a time she wasn't here."

"Your family has a way of making people feel apart of them." He smiles while looking around the table but then his eyes land on Abigail and they narrow. "Except her." Then he looks at my brothers. "And them."

I start laughing and he follows. "Max, they wouldn't bother torturing you if they didn't love you too." I try and reason with him.

Abigail must sense Max talking about her because she turns, smiles, points to his shirt and gives a thumbs up and starts cracking up. She gives me a wink and turns back to Nick.

"Yeah. Loved." His smile turns into grimace.

After dinner, we head out to the parking lot and say our goodbyes. Max and I head home with my grandma not far behind us in her car.

Once we're inside back at home, Grandma tells Max and I she's tired and is going on to bed and read and she'll see us tomorrow. I give her a kiss and Max and I make our way to our bedroom.

Max walks into our little bathroom but doesn't close the door. He changes into some basketball shorts hanging from a hook behind the door where I hang my gown and then starts brushing his teeth. While he stands by the sink, I grab my gown from the hook and change behind him. After dumping my clothes in the hamper, I reach around for my toothbrush and toothpaste. As I start brushing my teeth, our eyes meet in the mirror and he smiles before he leans down and starts rinsing his mouth. Once done, he walks out and turns on the lamp on the nightstand and crawls into bed. I spend a few moments studying him; the man who will become my husband. The sweet way he set up the entire proposal and included my whole family is something I'll never forget. I can't believe I'll get the chance to show him everyday how much I love him. I set my toothbrush down and leave the bathroom to join him in bed, frowning when I notice he's looking at his cell phone and shaking his head.

"What?" I ask as I climb in and scoot in closer to him to look over at the screen on his phone.

He's swiping the screen while reading texts and lightly chuckling. I briefly catch a picture of what looks like a noose and then jerk my head to him in question.

"Nash." He chuckles and keeps going.

I see one from Connor. *Yay! Tell Jaycee, I'll call her. We can plan our weddings together. Cake tastings and pick out invitations. Can't wait.*

Awe, that's nice but short lived as I see one from my dad. *If you hurt my daughter, they will never find your body.*

"Jesus Christ, Dad," I whisper.

There's one from my Aunt Savannah inviting all the girls to lunch for planning and then replies from the women with enthusiastic yes's. Then I see one from Violet, *So happy for y'all.*

Chase's name come up. *Good luck. You're a good guy, Blue. Happy for you both.*

"See? That was nice. Chase is a sweetheart." I tell him, confused when he bursts out laughing.

"Wait for it, Jaycee." He scrolls down and I see it's a video. He plays it and I gasp when a video of a bull being castrated pops up with the caption: *But break my sister's heart and you become the bull.* My hand flies to my mouth and I look at Max. He grins and turns the phone back to me. "I saved the best for last."

It's a still shot of the scene from Kill Bill when Kiddo is at the House of Blues and cuts off O-Ren's head with the caption: *Hurt my Sissy and...*from Abigail. My dad chimed in with, *that's my girl.*

"My family is crazy." I comment, a bit shocked. "You should probably run now. Don't wait. I'll help you pack." I start to exit the bed, heading for the closet to get his duffle bag, but Max grabs me from behind and buries his face in my neck, laughing.

"Jaycee, stop," he says as he laughs. "I have nothing to worry about because I won't hurt you," he promises as he kisses my neck. "Not ever but if for some reason I do, it won't be on purpose. I would never hurt my girl," he repeats in a whisper.

"That's sweet and all, but are you crazy?!" I screech and I try to pull away. "Get out, Max. While you can." Before I can finish, he pushes me back on the bed and straddles me.

"Jaycee, think of our millions of future kids. Do you really want to deny the world of a mixture of the Bradshaw and McGinty blood?" He starts kissing my neck.

I freeze. "Max, we can't do that to the world." I say in complete seriousness and he starts laughing. "No, really." I turn my head to give him better access to my neck. "We'll have to move. Buy an island to keep the craziness contained. Don't want it to spread into the normal population," I say and moan as he starts pulling my strap to my slip down and trails kisses down my shoulder. "And then the government will drop a nuclear bomb on our island."

"No, they won't." He chuckles. He grins at me, his

dimples on display before bringing his mouth back to mine. It's a kiss so passionate it ends our conversation or any talk for that matter, for the rest of the night.

CHAPTER EIGHTEEN

It's Friday, a week after the engagement and much to our surprise, our families are already talking about the wedding. Tonight, Max's mom, Ana, invited everyone over for dinner to discuss ideas and we're also going to get our first look at what my dad has planned for our home. All the family is here, except Johnny, but I hear he's on his way.

I'm sitting next to Max, watching everyone. Acer just brought Callie in from the garage. When she saw his motorcycle through the open garage door she started to skip and jump in excitement so Acer picked her up and sat her on the seat. She runs over to Connor and Bradley and tells them all about it. She's wearing the cutest baby pink and blue sundress with her brown boots. Her hair is hanging down today as she's forgone the bow for a pink cowboy hat. It's fallen off the top of her head and hanging around her neck from the stampede string. My heart warms watching her. She's family now and always.

While everyone's visiting, I pull Abigail outside in the backyard under the pretense of showing her Acer and Ana's garden, but really I want to talk about her and Nick.

As we're walking along the path, Abigail stops to smell the roses. They're beautiful. Max's dad has a serious green thumb. When she releases the flower she turns back to me and blows my mind.

"I love him so I'm moving to Lubbock to be with him." she says with a serious but dreamy smile.

"Huh?" is all I manage to get out.

"I love him. I want to be with him. I'm going to transfer to Texas Tech. They have an awesome agriculture department. I'm going to study Animal Science, specializing in the business side," she says on her last bit of air.

"Huh?" I repeat, still not processing.

"Nick's family. They own a small ranch or something, sissy, and he's going to be taking the helm soon. He's been working with his dad. He grew up on the ranch but was never much interested until recently. I'm going to help him." she explains almost pleading with me to understand.

"Dad?" I ask as I release a deep breath.

"I haven't told him yet but he'll need to understand. Jaycee, I almost died. We almost died. I'm not wasting any more time. I love him. I can't be without him." She says with watery eyes. "Dad will just have to suck it up. Plus, it's only a four maybe five-hour drive. We can come down on weekends or y'all can come up." she says as she starts pulling me towards Acer and Ana's garden.

"Abigail," I pull her to a stop. "If this is what you want, then I support you one hundred percent. I've seen you two together. The way you look at him. It's the way I look at Max. I get it."

I draw Abigail into a hug and then release her, but keep our arms linked as we start walking along the garden looking at the variety. All of a sudden, Abigail gasps and starts laughing. She's pointing at a section of potted plants, spices. As I lean in and get a closer look at the patch, I start laughing too. Yes, special spices.

"No way! Is that what I think it is?" I ask Abigail while still staring at the plants.

"Do you think it's locoweed? Spliff? Ganja? Reefer?" Abigail replies while laughing.

"What?" I start cracking up. "Yeah, I do."

"Then you would be right, sissy," Abigail says and then lets out a squeal when Nick comes up behind her and kisses her neck.

"What are you two up to?" Nick asks while looking Abigail up and down. "Your leg?" He frowns.

"It's fine, Nick. Remember the doctor said it's time for me to start using it again. It's just a little weak. I need to rebuild the muscle is all." She leans in and gives Nick a sweet kiss. "I'm fine. I promise."

I watch them thinking they look so good together and he is so caring towards her. I'm happy for her, for them. Voices behind us alert us to Johnny and Max's arrival.

"Hey, sugar," I call out as he gets closer. "Hi, Johnny," I greet him.

"Hey, sweetheart," Johnny says as he pulls me into a

hug. "Sorry I'm late. Yesterday we had something go down and today we had tons of paperwork."

"No. Don't be sorry. I'm just glad you made it. You're okay?" I say into his ear and he gives me a tight squeeze.

"I am now," he assures me.

When we pull back I turn to Max and wrap my arms around his waist. "How are things in there?" I ask hoping for the best.

"Our dads are talking politics. They're disagreeing while smiling and laughing. It's like watching for the impending train wreck but I was able to force myself to walk away," he tells me while wrapping his arms around me too.

"Wait, I thought they were both republicans," I say, confused.

"They are," he shakes his head.

"You're a cop right, Johnny?" Abigail asks Johnny.

Damn it, Abigail.

"Yeah. I'm a police officer. I serve on the S.W.A.T team," he replies smiling. Boasting a little.

"Wow, that's very impressive. So, yeah, have you ever busted people with drugs? Or do raids on people who, I don't know, manufacture in their home? Grow in their own yards or gardens or just hostage kinda stuff?" she asks while barely containing herself from jumping up and down.

"Anything, and all the time," he says and I can almost see the chip on his shoulder.

"Texas hasn't joined in with the other states legalizing pot yet, has it?" Abigail asks already knowing the answer.

"No. Not currently legal but I hear change is coming very soon. Why do you ask?" he replies cautiously. Just realizing he's being set up.

Max tenses behind me and at the same time, Johnny starts looking around the garden. Max turns us a little so he can get a better view, and he and Johnny both let their gazes roam over the area.

Oh, hell.

"Fuck," Max breathes out but also gives a quick chuckle.

"Fucking awesome, Mom and Dad," Johnny says in frustration, rubbing his hand over his face and looking back at the rest of us.

Nick is on the verge of tears laughing along with Abigail. Neither Max nor I can help the chuckling as Abigail coughs, clears her throat and continues her torment.

"So, um, what do you think that is right there?" She points to the section of potted plants.

"Oregano plants," Johnny replies dryly, without missing a beat and with a completely straight face.

"Yes, officer, sir. I see the oregano plants but look to the left. Those. What are those?" she says while trying not to laugh.

Without looking at the garden, Johnny replies. "Basil plants." He then raises one eyebrow at Abigail giving her a warning. A warning she completely ignores.

"Yes, Officer Johnny. I see the basil plants but you went too far to the left. Look back one plant. What kind of plants are those? The one between the oregano and basil," she asks.

"Pot. Those are pot plants," Acer says, causing as to jump; having not heard him walk up. Johnny shakes his head then drops his chin to his chest in defeat.

"I hate chemicals. I hate drug companies. Don't trust 'em. They all crooks. Granted, once in a blue moon they come up with something that can really help a sick person, but the rest of the time those bastards are killing us with their poison," he says as he leans down and checks the soil. "I prefer nature's remedy. I trust God and what He provides."

Can't argue with that.

Acer stands back up and wipes his hand off on his jeans. Now Johnny and Max look concerned.

"You okay, Pop?" Johnny ask frowning.

"We all got aches and pains. My knee hurts every now and again. Sometimes my elbow hurts. Every now and then I get a finger cramp," he says then grins.

"I get finger cramps too. They're awful," I blurt out.

"Me too, terrible pain," Abigail says, frowns and

shakes her head.

"Do you now?" Acer says trying not to laugh.

"Yes, it hurts..." I start to say but Abigail finishes for me.

"Now and again," she says and winks back at Acer and me.

"Finger cramps?" Max asks grinning at me.

"Sure," I raise my index finger and bend it back and forth at him until he finally laughs.

"I'm sure you all have pain but does it really reach to this level?" Johnny points to the pot plants.

"Pain is pain, Johnny," Abigail says to him. "Finger cramps are a full blown frown with a tear on the pain chart."

She manages to say with a straight face but Max and Nick are cracking up now and Acer is well on his way joining them.

"You know, Mom made pancit and lumpia so I'm walking away and pretending none of this ever happened," Johnny says as he starts back to the house.

"We're right behind you. That's why I came out. Need you all inside so we can say grace and eat," Acer tells us.

Once inside, we say grace and give thanks for food and family before sitting down to enjoy Ana's cooking. Midway through the meal, Uncle Brock's phone rings and he excuses himself to answer it. When he walks back in the room, he looks at Aunt Paige and then Callie who's sitting at the bar with Johnny, dunking a lumpia in soy sauce and vinegar with his help. She takes a bite and then squishes her face up and shakes her head. Johnny starts cracking up. I glance back at Uncle Brock and see that Aunt Paige has moved to his side. Whatever he says has her mouth dropping open in shock. He says something else and they both turn to walk back over to the table.

He starts to speak to everyone, but then looks back at Callie and stops. Ana gets up and without a word, picks up Callie from her seat beside Johnny.

"Callie, you want to come with me to grab some tomatoes from the garden? I need to get a few more and I'd love to have a helper." she asks while smiling at Callie. Aunt Paige sends her a grateful smile.

"Yay!" Callie squeals as Ana walks out the back door with Callie on her hip. Everyone has turned back from watching Callie and Ana and all eyes are on Uncle Brock.

"Tomorrow morning, if you would like to join us at the courthouse, nine o'clock, we'll be going through the official ceremony to adopt Callie." Uncle Brock tell us.

Whoops and cheers and happy tears start as everyone gets up from the table and comes forward to hug and congratulate them.

"This is wonderful. I thought you had at least another month before they waived the birth parents' rights. I can't believe how wonderful this news is," my grandma says.

Aunt Paige speaks up. "Brock just heard from Callie's social worker and was told that her mom passed away last night. They think it was a drug overdose. Apparently some paperwork turned up and it shows Callie's dad has passed too but they didn't say how."

I can see it's a bittersweet moment for my aunt and uncle.

"Her great aunt and her next of kin, waived rights and the judge told Callie's social worker he saw no reason to wait. He has an opening in the morning and told us to come in. You're all welcome to be there. We would love to share this moment with all of you." Aunt Paige looks at Johnny and Acer. "You're family now and are more than welcome to come too."

Acer smiles and replies. "I think Ana and I might just do that, darlin'."

"My captain gave me tomorrow off, so I'll be there." Johnny tells her.

The back door opens and Ana and Callie return. Callie has lifted the front of her dress up and is cradling three tomatoes in a makeshift pouch.

She looks up with big eyes and smiles. "Look, got me maters."

Everyone starts laughing as Uncle Brock carefully picks her up and kisses her on the head being careful not to smash her 'maters'.

"Love you, baby and those are some pretty tomatoes." He sets her back down.

"Love you, Daddy." She turns towards Aunt Paige but one of the tomatoes falls out and then another. "Mommy, ugh." She frowns. "My maters keep falling."

Aunt Paige kneels down in front of her and picks up her tomatoes and sets them back in her pouch. "I love you, Callie." She pulls her in for a soft hug and then sets back on her haunches and stares at Callie with a tear in her eyes.

"Love you, Mommy." she says and puckers her lips and gives her a kiss before carefully turning and slow as a snail starts back to the bar where Johnny is.

Johnny takes the tomatoes from her skirt and sets them next to her plate and then picks her back up and sets her on the stool before sitting back down on his. He hands her a lumpia, the tomatoes forgotten for the moment, and she dunks her lumpia in the tiny bowl holding the soy sauce, vinegar mixture and then hesitantly takes a small lick. Once she does, she scrunches up her face again and gives a whole body shiver from the strong sour taste. Laughs and chuckles can be heard all around as she goes back for more.

Johnny looks down at her as she goes back for even more and smiles. "Good stuff?"

"Mmmmmmmm," is all Callie says as she smiles and gives another full body shiver.

Yes, good stuff indeed.

CHAPTER NINETEEN

It's been a long day. Last night I called Nora Lee and asked if I could switch from the morning shift to the evening shift so I could be downtown at the courthouse in the morning. She offered me the entire day off but I felt bad so I told her I'd come in.

After going to Callie's adoption ceremony this morning the family went out for an early celebration luncheon at one of the places along the San Antonio River Walk. It's been a truly beautiful day.

When the judge asked Callie if she wanted my aunt and uncle to be her mommy and daddy, everyone held their breath. Callie walked up to Uncle Brock and raised her arms to be picked up. She poked him in the nose and said "my daddy" and then leaned into Aunt Paige to kiss her on the cheek, but it ended in a raspberry and said, "my mommy."

After the judge and everyone else in the courtroom stopped laughing, he granted the adoption and signed the papers. Before he left the courtroom, he came down off his bench and shook everyone's hand and squatted down in front of Callie to shake her hand but she wasn't having that, no, she walked up and gave him a big neck hug. Just like that, another one bites the dust.

Callie is now officially Callie Regan McGinty.

When I asked Aunt Paige, why she chose Regan, she told me Regan means "the King's child." The King being our Lord and Callie being a blessing from him, it seemed fitting. I love it. I think it's a beautiful name and fits her perfectly.

As the family walked along the river walk, I watched Callie, dressed in the cutest outfit of gold leggings with big brown polka dots on them, a soft yellow lacy dress with a cute brown tweed jacket with ruffles over top and a brown cloche hat and on her little feet, gold high top chucks with brown rhinestones that I know my aunt had made. Her golden locks were bouncing and swaying as she skipped along sidewalk getting too close to the edge of the water for comfort for the men. Chase couldn't take it any longer and scooped her up and sat her on his shoulders, eliciting squeals and giggles from Callie and a collective sigh from the men.

Now, I'm getting ready to leave work and head home to Max and my grandma. Picking up my cell phone to call home to see if I need to grab anything before I leave, I see a text from Ana, Max's mom. I shudder when I read she wants me to go with her to a pig farm to pick a pig for roasting at our post wedding celebration where all the family comes together and just kicks back in jeans instead of the formal wear. I'm almost more excited about that then the formal dinner. But I can't do the pig thing. Max is going to have to handle that. I push the button and call him and tell him about his mom's text.

"Max, if your Mom wants to roast a pig, that fine.

But you have to go with her to pick out the pig, not me. Please, help me out," I plead and he laughs.

"Okay, Jayc, I get it. When it's time to do the dirty deed, I'll take care of it." he says through his chuckles.

I shudder at the thought of looking a pig in the eye and then roasting it. "Okay, well, I'm leaving work, do we need anything?"

"No, we're good. Oh, and don't forget we're meeting your dad in the morning to go over the plans for the house." I can hear the smile in his voice.

"I'm so excited, Max." I'm practically jumping up and down with excitement. "Okay, I'm leaving now. See you in about ten minutes. Love you."

"Love you too, Jayc. See you in a few."

As I walk to the car, a figure approaches me so I stop and back up to where I'm under the lights from the store as I reach for my car keys.

"Hi, Jaycee, sorry to bother you but do you know who this might belong to?" A man's voice asks.

I tense when I see him come into the light. It's Jed. The customer I've seen in the store a couple of times that gives me the creeps. I step forward to see what he's holding in his hand. Taking it from him to get a closer look turns out to be a mistake. I start to panic and my heart starts racing.

"Where did you get this?" I whisper my voice full of confusion and fear.

He takes it back from me and closes his hand around it and puts it back in his pocket.

"So you do remember?" He asks and then grabs me.

He tries to pull me into the dark of the parking lot and I fight and scream for help while struggling, but he overpowers me and throws me to the ground. My head hits the blacktop hard and I find myself dazed, my vision goes blurry and my head starts pounding.

"Bitch, you're going to pay for what you did to her. A life for a life," Jed growls.

I try to keep my bearings and not pass out, but the pain in my head is intense. I vaguely make out another figure heading towards us.

"What the fuck? You?" Jed spits out.

I try to focus on what's happening, but my head is spinning, the pain increasing each time my head pounds

"Yeah, me. Hand it over." The second voice sounds familiar, but I can't place it

There's sounds of a scuffle, followed by feet hitting the pavement at a run.

"Yeah, behind Dan's Grocery, Jaycee McGinty has been attacked and is hurt." A hand swipes my hair from my face and cups my cheek gently, running his thumb softly across my cheek bone. He's kneeling next to me.

"Thank you," I mumble, but there's no reply. Sirens sound in the distance and only then does he finally speak.

"Gotta go, baby." He disappears from my side and moments later I see lights as the police and an ambulance and firetruck pull up. After the sirens turn off, I think I hear the roar of a motorcycle, but I can't be sure.

"Jayc!" Nash. He yells out my name and then drops down next to me. "What happened?"

I want to tell him but my head is pounding. "Nash, my head and my eyes," I moan.

I hear more voices; another man talking to Nash. "Hey, McGinty. I'm going to need you to step back a little so we can get to her."

"Yeah, okay." He tells him. "Jaycee, I'm going to be right here." He takes my hand and holds it tight. "But I need to step back a little and give them room. I'm going to call Dad and Blue, but I'll be right here."

"Kay." I moan out my reply as he releases my hand and moves away.

"Ms. McGinty, I'm Lieutenant Bryant. I'm with the fire department's paramedic' team. I'm just going to check you out, okay?" he says softly while pulling my hand away from my head. "You've got quite a bump there. Did you fall?" he asks while softly prodding the area.

"Hurts," I whisper.

"I'm sorry, Ms. McGinty. She's in too much pain to answer any questions. Let's get her loaded up and transport her. Call it in and let them know we're on our way." Lieutenant Bryant orders.

People are moving around me and then I feel a hand take mine. Nash is back.

"Hey, you're going to be okay. Dad's going to get Grandma and meet us at the hospital. Blue wouldn't wait. He'll be here in a minute," Nash tells me while rubbing his hand up and down my arm, soothing me.

Yet again I hear the sound of a motorcycle and I know Max is close. I know the sound of his bike like I know the sound of his voice and the feel of his touch. The sound is a relief but it's also making my head pound. The engine cuts off and his boot stomps running towards me. Tears of relief and pain fall from my eyes, down the sides of my face and into my hair. My Max, he'll help me.

"Love?" he says too loud and I wince.

"Blue, her head. Not too loud," Nash tells him.

"Jaycee, what happened? Jesus. What happened?" he barks.

"We need to get her prepped before we load her. You and Nash can ride or follow but let's get her in," Lieutenant Bryant says.

"Go head." I hear Nash say. "Want me to follow on your bike?"

"Yeah, thanks, Nash," Max answers.

"Ms. McGinty, we're going to lift you onto a gurney and load you up, but first I need to put this brace around your neck and take your vitals. I know you're in pain so I'm going to give you a shot with some strong pain medicine."

He rubs something cold along my hand. "I need to get an IV started as well. You're going to feel a pinch but then your pain should start subsiding a little." Lieutenant Bryant explains.

I feel the pinch but it's nothing compared to the pounding in my head. It starts to sting and then I feel warmth spread through my body and I relax, as my pain begins to subside.

"We'll give it a couple of seconds to kick in and then we're going to start to do this as quickly and as painless as possible." Lieutenant Bryant says as he taps my hand gently. "Better?"

"Yes," I hiss out and smile wide as the pain fades even more.

"Let's get her loaded." Lieutenant Bryant says.

Everything else happens fast. All at once, something wraps around my neck and the band of the blood pressure cuff tightens around my arm.

"All good." I hear someone say.

Then hands are lifting me. Lots of hands. Surely I'm not *that* heavy that it takes *that* many hands to lift me. Someone nearby lets out a laugh.

"No, you're not heavy, Ms. McGinty. Just didn't want to jostle you too much." Lieutenant Bryant says.

Oh, I said that outloud? That's funny.

I feel myself being rolled and then I'm inside the back of the ambulance. Nash tells Max he'll meet us at the hospital. The ambulance doors slam shut and then I start swaying a little as the ambulance moves.

"I'm cutting the lights back here. Call it in and tell them it's a code two but we're coming in cold. No siren. Just light it up if you need to." Lieutenant Bryant orders to whoever is up front.

"Yes, sir." The person replies. Conversation continues around me, but I have a hard time making out what they're saying.

"What happened?" Max asks but I can tell he's not talking to me. His hand takes mine, being careful of the needle in my arm.

"Dispatch got a call of a woman being attacked behind Dan's Grocer. That's all the information they gave before cutting the call," Lieutenant Bryant tells Max. "Got there and found her lying where you saw her. She has a pretty good bump on her head. Probably has a level two concussion. I don't think she lost consciousness."

"Attacked? I knew she was hurt; but attacked?" Max voice radiates with anger.

"That's what the caller reported but whoever called was gone when we got there. She was alone." Lieutenant Bryant tells Max.

"He didn't stay? Leave a name?"

My pain is now a dull pounding so I try to respond. I lick my dry lips and tell them who the caller was.

"A customer, Jed, Jedidiah, he tried to kill me. The

one I told you about Max. He said a life for a life. I don't know what the means, Max, but we struggled and I fell. He started to come at me but I saw someone stop him and then call 911. It was Rocky. He called. Rocky stopped Jed. He's alive, Max. Rocky is alive. I saw him at Jacala's too." That's the last thing I say before I let the effects of the medicine take over as the adrenaline leaves my body.

CHAPTER TWENTY

My eye is pried open and a light is shined into it. What an asshole. I try slapping away the hands but when I reach to do it, the other eye is opened and I'm blinded again. Jesus, what the hell? I change directions and try to slap at the hands again but they've moved again. I let out a deep sigh of defeat and drop my arms and hands back down to my sides.

"Sorry, Jaycee but I have to check you over." A familiar voice says with momentary humor. It's Dr. Kilpatrick. I open my eyes and turn towards his voice. He looks pissed off as he probes around my head.

"You got a nice bump going, Jaycee. And a concussion. I'm sure it hurts so we're going to give you something for pain and check on you every couple of hours. I examined you and all but your head looks okay. Anything else I should know?"

He almost looks scared as he waits for the answer. He knows I was beaten and raped the last time I was brought here.

"No. Just my head, Dr. Kilpatrick," I try to smile.

"Okay, good." He releases a deep breath. "Sergeant Bradshaw is about to lose his mind so I'm going to send him in first but the detectives and sheriff are here too. Do you feel like talking?" he asks. He glances to the side and its the first time I realize there's someone else in the room. Corporal Blass.

"Hi." I say softly, feeling slightly embarrassed to be here again.

"Hi, Jaycee. How's your head feeling?" she asks and walks closer.

"Better, I think." I whisper. "Max?"

"Let me get him for you." she offers. Dr. Kilpatrick writes in my chart as she leaves the room. A few moments later, Max and my dad walk in.

"Sweetheart, what happened?" Dad asks as he carefully touches my face.

"Jed, this customer, was waiting for me in the parking lot. He asked for my help. Asked me if I knew who something he had belonged to. When I took it from him to get a closer look, I recognized it. That's when he attacked me. Told me I was going to pay. An eye for an eye." I start to cry. Max hasn't said a word; his body is vibrating with rage. Shit. He's going to freak out.

"Jed? The guy you told me about? What did he have Jaycee?" Max grinds out through closed teeth. I swallow hard and wipe my eyes. This is too much for him.

"It was the necklace Rocky gave me the night I went to dinner at his parents' house. The one Kelly ripped from my neck. It's a Celtic cross with an emerald in the center. I have no idea how or why he had it." I answer cautiously. My breathing becomes heavy as I recall what happened next.

"I tried to fight him but he was strong. I fell and hit my head and it was instant pain. Everything was blurry, but I could still see images. I saw Jed walking towards me and I knew I was in deep trouble; but then someone else arrived. I don't know what happened after that. The next thing I remember is Rocky leaning down, checking me and then calling 911. He stayed until the sirens could be heard and then he said he had to go." A sob escapes from my throat. "I'm so sorry. So sorry."

"Jesus, love, stop crying. Why in the fuck would you be sorry?" He climbs next to me on the bed and pulls me to him gently. "I'm so fucking sorry. I should have gone down there. I should have made sure you got to your car safe. You usually work days, I wasn't thinking. This is my fault."

"It's no one's fault except who did this." Dad tells us. He doesn't get a chance to say anymore as the door to my room opens and in walks a very pissed off trio. *Oh, shit.*

Sheriff Cullens, Captain Walters and Sergeant Taylor look like they have murder on their mind.

Sheriff Cullens approaches me and gives me a kiss on the forehead. "Hey, darlin. How you feeling?" he asks.

"I'm fine." I answer, sadness in my eyes.

"This shit needs to end, gentleman," Dad demands.

"We know, Stone. We know. How are you, Jaycee?"

Captain Walters asks as he comes forward and stands next to Max.

"It hurts a little but better than before." I say and then turn to Sergeant Taylor who's reading something on his phone.

"Hey, Jaycee," he says as he puts his phone away and walks over to my bed. I smile at him as he looks at Captain Walters before he speaks. "Max and I talked while you were out and I need to get a few things straight so answer as best you can. So, let me just ask first, are you saying Jedidiah Price is the one who attacked you?"

"Jedidiah, Jed, yes. I don't know his last name," I reply.

"I just got a message from another detective who answered a call about a shooting three blocks from Dan's Grocer. A caller reported hearing two gunshots and when the police answered the call, they found a man, dead. He's been identified as Jedidiah Price. After a quick background check, it was found he was connected to Kelly Price. She was his sister."

"What the hell is going on? You know something. You need to tell us so we can protect, Jaycee." Max demands.

Captain Walters and Sargent Taylor exchange a glance with Sheriff Cullens. Sheriff Cullens drags over a couple of chairs and has my dad sit in one as he takes the other. Sergeant Taylor takes a seat on the small couch across from the bed and starts explaining what the police think is going on.

"We've learned quite a bit more concerning Rocky Jennings and Dr. Jennings, since we last spoke. It's pretty scary stuff. Basically, Dr. Jennings and few other people, high up in city government were trying to create a new narcotic drug. A pain medication. It seems to have started out with the pure intentions of finding something that would help people, but then the greed for money and power took over. Looks like early on they tried the honest approach and applied for grant money, worked with the FDA and even presented theories and research they'd done to large drug companies."

Well, that's not too scary but I feel it coming. I can feel the room shift and change. Darkness and anger is now radiating off the three of them. My dad sits up straight and leans forward with his elbows on his knees, waiting like Max and I. Captain Walters take in a deep breath and releases it before taking over where Sargent Taylor left off.

"When nothing panned out in those avenues, that's when things took a turn for the worse. They decided to continue trying to create the drug by selling it on the streets or to the cartel if need be to make their money. When the cartel got involved and set them up with a lab, they went to work. When the cartel started feeling like they were getting jerked around, Dr. Jennings and the others pushed things forward fast. They stepped up testing. Here's the thing," Captain Walters lowers his head for a moment so Sheriff Cullens finishes up.

"It seems they didn't use normal or more

traditional methods for testing. They were using humans. Unknowing and unwilling humans. It made some of them very sick with heart and kidney issues, muscular issues, mental issues, anger, memory loss, paranoia. In extreme cases, some of their "patients" died. They did this to people they knew. They were secretly drugging them through food, tampering with medicine, injections. From the evidence, Rocky was allowing his father to use him for testing. We're surmising it was to protect his brother and mother. To keep the focus on himself and away from them." His expression is grim.

A lump grows in my throat, my nose starts to tingle and my eyes turn glassy with unshed tears. I cough to clear my throat and confirm what they're saying.

"You're saying Dr. Jenning's poisoned his own family? Is he responsible for Lina Jenning's being in a wheelchair?" The horror that her condition could be a direct result of her own husband's madness is almost too much to bear.

"What kind of man does that to his wife and sons?" Dad asks in an angry whisper.

"No man, Stone. No man would ever do that to anyone much less his wife and children." Captain Walters' replies.

"Now that Dr. Jennings is dead and not poisoning Lina and Rocky, will they be okay? Return to what they were before? Whoever they were before?" Max asks.

"We don't know yet. First we need to find Rocky.

We had a feeling he might have survived when a list of high profile names allegedly involved with this mess along with evidence kept turning up. Jaycee confirmed it. We can possibly get him some help. We have all the proof of what they did to him. His torture has been going on since his early teens. Mrs. Jennings, her torture, longer mostly because she was there the years Rocky was away with the military but when he came back, it seems Dr. Jenning's stopped testing on her. At least a few months before his murder anyway. She is in Lubbock with Lincoln. Texas Tech has a medical annex school there that might be able to help her along with her physicians. Rocky, I don't know exactly what effects this testing had on him or if it reversible. We need to find him. He's out for vengeance," Sargent Taylor tell us.

"Do you blame him?" Dad asks.

"If I wasn't an officer of the law, I'd help him exact his justice." Sheriff Cullens adds his thoughts.

"We all would," Captain Walters adds. "But we cannot allow him to perform acts of vigilantism."

"Sure you can." Max finally speaks and his answer surprises me.

"Max, are you okay?" I ask and lean into him.

"Fine, love." He rubs the top of my head. "How are you feeling?"

"It hurts, but better," I tell him, forcing a smile.

"I say let him have his vengeance. Whoever did

what they did to him, they're ultimately the reason he hurt Abigail and Jaycee. They deserve to pay. They all do." Max says.

"Yes, but what reason he had for doing what he did to Abigail and Jaycee, may not apply here. If he knows what he's doing now, when he's caught he can't use that as an excuse. He's probably going to prison." Sergeant Bradshaw.

"Doesn't it?" Sheriff Cullens asks. "Drugs could still be missing with him. We don't know."

Like I'm having an out of body experience I agree with Sheriff Cullens. "Does he? Does he really? Because if that's true, then I hope he seeks and gets his revenge and I hope he gets away."

Max looks at me in shock. I know he's thinking about my feelings for Rocky now knowing his behavior wasn't of his doing. I can see it and feel it in his touch. He's pulling away.

"Max, I love you. I always have. I thought I loved Rocky, but no, it didn't reach the level of what I feel for you. Even if Rocky was perfect, it would be you, and only you, but there were times I saw the little boy in him and that's who my heart hurts for. They should have to pay." I turn to Sergeant Taylor. "The list. How many names are on the list?"

Captain Walters looks at Sergeant Taylor and Sheriff Cullens before he answers. "Eight. A total of eight names are on the list."

"Two are dead and one turned himself in this morning, a doctor. He came in with his lawyer and he wants to make a deal. He's willing to give us his documentations of the work he was involved in and also names from other major and minor players. The ones on the list, they were the biggest of all. Another doctor has gone into hiding, a politician is denying any involvement, a law enforcement officer was listed and is being dealt with first by Internal Affairs and another one of the major players ran back to his compound in Mexico." Captain Walters tells us.

"We strongly believe that Rocky is hunting the members of this list. We have no idea how or when he'll strike next. One of the deaths was by a woman we think he was involved with. That turned into a murder suicide." Sergeant Taylor fills us in.

"A woman? What woman?" My head starts to pound. I don't know if it's from my injury or all the information, but my dad notices and puts a stop to it all.

"Okay, enough. Jaycee needs to rest." he says and stands.

"He's right, honey. We'll talk soon, Jaycee. Get some rest." Captain Walters says and gives my shoulder a squeeze before he heads for the door with Sergeant Taylor following him.

"Try to get some rest, Jaycee. I'm thinking Rocky means you no more harm but just in case, I want you to stay with someone at all times. You should be safe here. I'm going to alert hospital security to keep an eye on your room and when you get home, I'll arrange for drive-bys every half hour or so." Sheriff Cullens says and gently kisses me on the head.

"I'll be back in a bit, sweetheart. I need to make some calls and I'll stop by the nurses' station on my way out and ask for more pain medication." Dad says, sharing a look with Max before walking out.

Before I can say anything to Max, he shushes me. "Love, later. Just rest."

Over the next few hours, Max and I doze off and on between the nurses coming in to check on me. The next afternoon, I head home with a prescription for pain pills and aftercare instructions. Other than a slight throb and feeling overwhelmed by what was shared with us by the police, I'm feeling okay.

After some dotting by my grandma, Max takes me to the bathroom in our room. He turns the shower on and while the water is warming he begins taking my clothes off. After he undresses me, he quickly undresses and steps in, adjusting the water and shower head before pulling me in with him. He gently washes my hair and my body before washing himself. When he's done, he pulls me to him, my back to his front and he just holds me. We stand that way, quiet, until the water starts to cool.

He grabs a towel from the shower door and dries me off and then wraps me up tight and kisses me on the head and wraps me up tenderly. We walk back into the room and rather than trying to go through my clothes, he just grabs one of his shirts from the closet and puts it on me and starts buttoning it up. Once I'm dressed, he puts his hands on my hips but doesn't meet my eyes. I can't take it. I need him to look at me.

"Max?" I whisper.

"No, Jaycee. Just, no." he says, shaking his head.

"Please, you're scaring me." I say but he stays silent. Finally, I say what I know he needs to hear. I have to let him go. "It's too much, isn't it? Do you need to leave me? I don't blame you, Max. I'm sorry." I try to pull back as his head snaps up.

"What?" His eyes search my face as guilt forms in his eyes. "Never ever, love." he assures me.

He pulls me to the bed and sits me on the edge while he walks over and grabs a pair of boxers and some jeans. He pulls them on but doesn't button them before he kneels in front of me.

"I'm not going anywhere. I...I just, fuck, I still hate him, Jaycee. I still fucking hate him but I feel so fucking sorry for him too. I keep seeing you in that hospital bed and hearing you cry when you found out you'd been pregnant. Knowing he raped you and I just don't know. I still want him to fucking burn. I want the others to burn with him. I want him to take those bastards to hell and go with them; but I have a small voice telling me to fucking forgive him. Either way, I feel he's always going to be a threat," he finishes, confusion written all over his face.

I slide from the bed and kneel in front of him and put my hands on his chest as I look up in his eyes and attempt to gather my thoughts before I speak. "For me, Max, I want so badly for him to have peace after hearing what he went through. For someone to heal his heart. For him to be rescued." I can tell he still doesn't get it. "Max, I was taught to forgive." I bow my head before looking back at him.

"I almost died at birth but I lived. I lost my mom but gained my grandparents. I almost died in that field but then I opened my eyes and saw you." I push him till he falls on his back and I lay down on top of him.

"Why would I hate him? I needed him to get to you. He was my path to you. Everything I've been through was so I could get here, right here." I smile and touch his face as his hands go to my hips and squeeze. "I love you so much more than any hate I could ever possibly feel for him. I'd rather have my heart full of love for you than my head full of anger for him. I asked God in my prayers to take my anger from me and I've had peace for a while now. I still hurt and sometimes have a flashback, but I know in time they'll fade. I know I saw something in him. Something good. He just didn't know what or how to deal with it. It's him that caused all this pain and harm but it may not be his fault. I see Lina and Lincoln Jennings and I know I saw bits of the same kind of good in him that we all see in them but that doesn't mean I want him or love him more than I would any other child of God. It's like people who steal food when they're hungry. Do we fault them or show them compassion? Max, Rocky, he was starving for love and he took it. As he was my path to you, I feel we all were his path to somewhere better too. I know whoever he was before is

212

there, but I'm still terrified of him." I drop my head on Max's chest. "Give yourself peace, sugar, love me more than your hate for him."

His hands tighten on my hips as we continue to lay there. Finally, he taps my hips so I raise up and straddle him. He sits up and I wrap my arms around his neck and my legs around his waist and lean in and give him a kiss I hope conveys how much I love him. He wraps one hand tight around my waist and with the other pushes up off the ground and stands.

"I'll try. Come on, love. Let's sleep." he pulls the covers back with me still clinging on like a monkey.

I can't help but let out a soft giggle before I tell him. "I was quite capable of getting up by myself, sugar bear." I kiss his cheek. "But thanks for lift." I joke trying to lighten the mood.

He looks at me grim and serious. "He's still out there, Jaycee. He's unpredictable."

I give him a sad smile. "I know."

He looks in my eyes and gives a quick nod before laying down on his back and pulling the covers over us. I lay down on his chest and place my ear over his heart and close my eyes. Max starts to pray and I lie still asking God to hear him so he can have peace too. We fall asleep like that but when I wake up, he's gone.

CHAPTER TWENTY-ONE

When I wake up, I notice a soreness and slight throb still present so I softly brush my hair and teeth, throw on some jeans but keep Max's shirt on. Even though it's way too big I love it. I take the front tails tie them in a knot at my belly button before and grab my phone to call work. But first I walk into the kitchen, take down a mug and pour some coffee before searching for Max and Grandma. I find them sitting on the porch.

I sit down next to Max and put my coffee and phone next to me on the table. He doesn't say anything, but reaches over and takes my hand. After a few minutes, he finally looks over and smiles.

"Good news," he tells me.

Grandma's rocking chair squeaks as she gets up and start towards the door giving us privacy. Once she's inside, Max gives me a small peck on the lips.

"What?"

"My enlistment is up next month and I've decided not to reenlist. Going to stay here all the time." He looks back towards the front yard.

Good news? This doesn't seem like good news? I thought he loved his job. And he's been in a long time just to walk away. He's doing it for me and I can't let him.

"Max, I have few conditions before we actually go through with our wedding." I wait to be acknowledged. Once he squeezes my hand, I go on.

"First, don't lie to me. I know this is not good news." His face fills with grief and sorrow. "Max, everything is going to be okay. I'm going to be okay. I grew up with military men all around me. I know the life and love the life. I always dreamed of being a military wife like my grandma and once we're married that dream will come true." He doesn't respond for a few seconds but finally says,

"I'll have to leave. Deploy. I don't know how often or how long. There's still a war. You don't hear about but it's still there. Soldiers getting hurt and killed. There will be times I have to go and that means leaving you," he says somberly.

"Max, they need you; I'll be here waiting. You can't leave the military. How long have you been in? Eleven years? You're an E7, right?" I ask.

He shrugs his shoulders.

"Max, someone does not stay in that long if they don't intend to make it a career. It's only nine more years at the most. You're almost there." I crawl in his lap and he wraps his arms around my waist, pulling me close and resting his chin on my head as I snuggle into his chest.

"I'm tougher than you think," I whisper.

"I know you're tough, love. It's just, I'm not." He

pulls me closer and I wrap my arms around him and hold him tight.

I realize I'll have to work on this. I don't want him to give up on something I know he loves for something that may or may not happen.

"It sucks but I have to go into work for a while and talk with my commander. I'm going to ask for an extension on my leave and talk to him about re-upping." I start to say something but he shakes his head. "I'll play it by ear. That's all I can promise." He sighs and stands us up. "Sheriff Cullens is coming over with one of his deputies to stay with you and your grandma while I'm gone."

As soon as he says that, I hear a car pulling up the drive. It's my Aunt Paige and I'm guessing Callie is with her. When she stops her car, she gets out and waves at us.

I smile and wave back and start to laugh when I hear Callie calling out, "Knuckle Max!" I smile wider because she's the only other person besides me that calls him Max and I love that. After Aunt Paige gets her out of her car seat and sets her down, she runs to Max and he picks her up swings her to his hip. She does the thing she only does with him, she puts her little hands on the sides of his face and pulls it to hers. After she takes a deep breath to calm down she looks right at him, "Hi." I watch as his eyes go soft like they only do for her. I can tell, Max to her is what my Uncle Duke is to me.

"Hi, Princess," he says as his eyes go even softer.

We head inside and sit down in the living room as

my grandma comes in with her purse and car keys in her hand.

"There's an emergency with some new choir robes at the church. Apparently the new ones are, 'boring'." she says using air quotes and babbling. "There are threats of boycotting this week's service," she says while looking in the bowl on the table by the door for her keys that are already in her hand. "Some of these women, I swear they wouldn't be happy if you gave them one of the Queen of England's robe to wear during the service." She huffs and keeps looking as Max, Aunt Paige and I share a glance and grin. "I mean its church for Christ's sake, not the red carpet." She starts out of the room, puts her purse down on the table and starts looking through it with her keys still in her hand. "There's twelve of them up there sharing the spotlight for less than five minutes. It's ridiculous. Their singing," she shudders, "they all think they're Maria Callas or someone. And Lord forgive me, but when they try to harmonize like they're the Celtic women, they sound like a bunch diseased coyotes howling a death cry. Half the congregation leaves for the restroom when it's time for the anthem, children and grown men cry, I just don't know anymore."

We all watch and wait. Finally, she stills and pulls her hand out of her purse and lifts the one holding the keys and just stares of them. "They're driving me insane." She throws up her hands and laughs. "Come here, sweetheart." she calls out to Callie, who runs up to her. "I'll be back soon and then we'll have some ice cream, okay?" Grandma smiles as Callie lets out a squeal of joy.

She picks her purse back up and then starts out the door but then stops again. She reaches for the top of her head and feels her sunglasses there, pulling them down. "I have some sanity left." she declares with a smile as she closes the door behind her.

As her car leaves, Sheriff Cullen's car comes up the drive. Max walks over to me and pulls me to him. "I'll only be gone a couple of hours, I hope. Just stay inside okay?" he tells me as he kisses me. He doesn't forget about Callie and makes sure to give her a peck on the cheek as well.

Max walks outside and meets Sheriff Cullens and the deputy I've never seen by their car. The three men talk for a few minutes before Max walks over to where his bike is and hops on and drives off. Aunt Paige takes Callie into the kitchen and I can hear them talking about eating a good lunch before Grandma gets back and she has her ice cream. Sheriff Cullens and the deputy are still outside talking in low voices.

Sheriff Cullens give the deputy a nod and starts up the front steps of the porch. My hand flies out and a scream catches in my throat as I watch the deputy pull his gun out, aim it at the Sheriff's back and fire twice. He falls to the steps and blood starts to spread across the porch. My heart pounds out of my chest and I'm frozen in fear as I watch the deputy pull out his cell phone and make a call. As he's talking, our eyes lock and he knows I've seen everything. When I hear Callie's giggle come from the kitchen I finally come back to myself and realize he is probably going to kill me and probably them too. I know I can't let that happen. I have to protect Callie and get help and then I remember the alarm. I slam the door shut and lock it, looking back out the window to see him shaking his head and laughing. I hit the emergency buttons on the alarm panel and then grab the house phone as I run into the kitchen where Aunt Paige and Callie are sitting at the table. Finding strength I didn't know I had to try to save us I move to protect us till help comes and make myself focus and not panic.

"Now! Get her now and let's go." I whisper yell and point to Callie. My aunt gets up and runs around the table and grabs Callie, pulling her close. Fear flashes on Callie's face; she senses trouble.

"What's going on?" Aunt Paige exclaims.

I grab her arm and start pulling her through the house. "The deputy. He shot Sheriff Cullens and then made a call." I open my bedroom door and look around for anything to use as a weapon. When I see nothing I tell Aunt Paige "I've hit the alarm. They should be calling any second. Help should be here soon." I reassure them. When nothing happens I bring the phone up and dial 911. I put the phone to my ear and when I hear nothing I close my eyes and start to cry but when I hear a tiny sniffle I look over at Callie and see she's watching me and is starting cry too. I take a deep breath and try to reassure her with a smile before I turn to check the alarm panel, dread fills me when I find it dead. *Shit!* They must have done something to it too. Before I have time to process that, there's banging on the front door and a man's voice calls out my name. I push Aunt Paige and Callie into the back of the room where the closet is and push them in. I drop down when I hear more banging, getting on my hands and knees intending to crawl towards the kitchen and find a knife, anything to protect us.

"Stay here!" My aunt grabs my leg. "No, Jaycee. Stay here with us." she pleads.

"Jaycee? I need to speak with you for a moment. No worries though. I didn't come for you. I came for her." he says and I can hear footsteps walking around the front porch. "Head around back. Check the windows and the doors. We don't have much time. They'll be trying to contact the sheriff and when he doesn't answer, they'll send back up." He barks orders to someone else.

I look back at Aunt Paige and she's shaking her head. "What's he talking about? Me? He wants me?"

"Jaycee, I need that adorable little girl. I won't hurt her but I need her to draw out your dead boyfriend. You can have her back as soon I kill him for good," he says.

What the hell does Callie have to do with this? Aunt Paige pulls Callie close. Callie doesn't know what's going on but she's caught on that she needs to stay quiet. She's clinging on to my aunt's neck.

"Your cell?" She shakes her head.

"I left it in the car." Her eyes start to tear up.

"Mines out on the front porch. We're just going to have to protect ourselves and fight back until help comes," I tell her. "If helps comes," I say softly to myself as I look back at the door. "Stay in here and close the door. You need to keep Callie hidden. I'm going to lock and close the outer bedroom door. I'm going to get a knife from the kitchen and I'll be right back."

The words are barely out of my mouth before loud thumps sound from the front door. They're breaking it down. "Now stay hidden in here" I say harshly and Aunt Paige's eyes tear up as she holds Callie even tighter and squats in the very back of the closet. I look at Callie who has her face buried in my aunt's neck and I lean over and quickly give her a kiss before turning, kneeling and leaving them. I'm terrified but I will do whatever it takes to protect Callie. I crawl past the windows and once I'm out of the room, I lock it from the inside. It's not going to stop them from getting in, but it might buy us a little more time.

I stand up and run as fast as I can to the kitchen and grab the biggest knife I can from the butcher's block and then run into my grandma's room. If anything, I can try to draw them away from Callie. I push myself flush against the wall as I hear footsteps making their way from the back of the house to the front. Terror makes my head spin as the front door opens the sound of footsteps fills the otherwise silent house.

"Jaycee, let makes this easy. I just need the little girl."

"Over my fucking dead body, asshole." I say under my breath.

He goes on. "I'm sure you know what's going on by now." His footsteps tell me he's getting closer and I grip the handle of the knife so hard my knuckles turn white. "Your boyfriend is going around killing people and I'm not really in the mood to die anytime soon and neither is my boss, so we need some assurance. That would be Callie." he explains.

Ha! I think in my head. *I can't wait for Rocky to find you and I hope makes you suffer. And what the hell does Callie have to do with this? She's just a child. Why is he coming after a little girl?*

I hear a motorcycle in the distance. I'm relieved and alarmed at the same time. Max, I don't want him to get hurt. But as it gets closer and closer, I know it's not Max.

"Ah, here's Rocky now, Jaycee," he says and I hear him harshly whisper to the others. "Find her or we're all dead." Running footsteps echo in the hallway and I fall to floor and crawl under the bed as far back against the wall as I can.

"Buck?" Rocky bellows. "This is between us. You and I. You want me, I'm here."

"Rocky, got to say, not trusting you since you turned on all of us. You used to be one of us. Now, you come after us? Kill us?"

"Yeah, that's right, Buck. Going to kill each and every one of you." Rocky says calmly, as if discussing the weather. "Won't rest till you're all burning in hell for what you did."

"You're going to burn with us, Rocky. Remember that." The deputy he calls Buck yells.

"Yeah, I am. And I'm okay with that." More gunshots sound and I cover my ears to block out the sound, my heart pounding so hard I can feel it in my throat. My breathing is too loud; I try to take a steadying breath, but I almost scream when someone walks into the room. The booted feet walk through the room; I can see the barrel of a shotgun aimed at the ground.

I hold my breath as he stops right in front of the bed. Sweat is dripping down my face and running into my eyes; burning them. He shifts positions and although I'm not sure what I'm going to do, I get my knife ready to swing. The bed skirt flies up and I push back out the other side and stand; ready to run.

I come face to face with a killer. The deputy. He smiles and raises the shot gun at me. I can tell he's deciding on whether to kill me or not when more gunfire breaks out in the backyard. At first he doesn't react. He stares at me and then tilts his head for me to follow him. Another round of gunfire erupts, but he keeps the gun on me.

He lets out an annoyed breath, then smiles and winks at me. "This isn't over. As long as he's alive, they'll keep coming for her." This time he turns and rushes out the door. A few seconds later, several car doors slam followed by the squeal of tires.

Everything goes quiet as I back into the corner still holding the knife. Taking a few calming breaths, I slowly start to the door. I take a peek towards the kitchen and nothing. Sirens suddenly sound in the distance. Lots and lots of sirens. There's still no movement so I take a chance and start through the house. I say a prayer as I try to open the door and find it still locked. I softly knock and call out to them cautiously. When nothing happens, I use the knife to jimmy the latch and pull the door open. The closet is still closed so I make my way to it and again cautiously call out; not wanting them to think I'm one of the bad guys.

"Aunt Paige? Callie?" My voice is shaky and hoarse and ends on a sob. Finally, I manage to somewhat yell to them. "Callie? Aunt Paige? It's okay, I think." My eyes dart around the room, relieved when it looks like nothing was touched. They never got this far. "You can come out."

The door slowly opens and Aunt Paige comes out holding a shaken Callie. She sees me and starts crying and reaches out for me. I know how worried and scared she must have been. I take her from Aunt Paige and hold her close and try to soothe her. The sirens are getting closer, we start to walk to the front of the house when a man appears from around the corner; pointing a gun at us. We freeze in place.

"I just need her." He points to Callie and I tighten my grip on her as I take a few steps back.

"Why?" I ask. "She's a child. What could you possibly want with her?" An evil smile stretches across his face.

"You don't know who she is?" He chuckles. "Let me rephrase my question. Do you know who this little girl belongs to?" When we all stay quiet, he laughs.

As he laughs, a shadow comes up behind him and a gun is pointed at his head. "You should have left with them." The newcomer speaks up. The man freezes, all color draining from his face. "Jaycee, you and Callie turn around. You too, Paige, turn around. Callie, cover your ears, baby."

I'm frozen as Rocky comes into view. His hair is long, his beard full. He gives Callie a small, sad smile. She's staring at him and she doesn't seem afraid; it's almost like she knows him. I look closer at Callie and then back to Rocky. Their eyes. There's something about their eyes...

"Jaycee, baby, I need you to turn around and Callie, cover your ears." Rocky repeats.

I start to protest right as the man makes a move towards us with his gun. As quick as I can, I drop to the ground and cover Callie. Aunt Paige does the same as one gunshot is fired and then there's nothing but silence. Too terrified to move, I stay down, covering Callie's body with mine.

Footsteps start towards us and I look up as Rocky steps over the man's body and reaches down to help me up. I hesitate, but then tentatively reach for his hand, keeping my eyes locked on his, which are starting to tear up. As I make my way to my feet with Callie in my arms, he breaks eye contact with me and smiles down at Callie. Catching me off guard, she reaches out her arms and falls into him. He catches her and holds her close for a few moments and then pulls back. Aunt Paige and I are completely blown away as we watch them together.

Their hair is different, but their eyes, they're exactly

the same.

Callie looks down and frowns. Rocky pushes her back into my arms so hard we fall to the ground. Two more gunshots fire off followed by shouts and the sound of running feet. I start to panic, looking around for somewhere to hide until I see Max. I almost weep in relief. The police, my family and Max are here. Rocky falls against the wall with his gun hanging down at his side.

Callie squirms to get free of my hold.

"No, baby." He gasps, shaking his head; she pushes off me again trying to get down but I hold her tight. All the men flood the room and point their guns at Rocky.

"No, he saved us!" Aunt Paige yells out.

"He protected us," I whisper.

"I'm sorry," he says to me. "So sorry for everything. For our baby." Tears start dropping from my eyes as I see that he's sincere in his remorse.

"I know," I say.

He looks around at everyone. "I wanted to make it right."

Bringing his gaze back to Callie and I, his gun drops to the floor. Callie cries and pushes so hard that I almost drop her as she jumps from my arms and runs to him. Bradley kneels down and grabs her and holds her despite her continued struggles.

"Callie, go back to your aunt Jaycee, baby," his breathing is heavy and he starts to turn pale. Max tucks his gun in the back of his jeans as Nash and Jesse do the same.

"Fuck, he's been hit," Max hiss's, moving to Rocky's side.

Hit? Where? I look down at Rocky's shirt and a small amount of blood is starting to form. Jesse grabs one of his arms as Nash takes his other.

"Jake, grab some towels," Max calls out.

Uncle Brock makes his way to Callie and takes her from Bradley. "You okay, honey?" he asks as he checks her over and then yanks Aunt Paige to ensure she's not hurt. "Jesus Christ, I've never been so scared in my life."

Max, Jesse and Nash help Rocky to lie down on the ground as Jake comes forward with towels. My dad and Uncle Duke make their way over to me. The pool of blood is spreading under Rocky, its red coloring making the situation more real. I gasp as Uncle Brock turns Callie so she doesn't see it, but it's too late and she starts crying.

"Down! Down! GO! GO! PWEASE! PWEASE!" she screams and begs, her cries turning to wails. Uncle Brock swears as he puts her down and she runs to Rocky.

She crawls up next to him and lays her head on his shoulder as he reaches and pulls her closer with one hand, caressing her hair with the other. Max takes the towels from Jake and lifts Rocky enough to get the towels underneath him, applying pressure to his wounds. A noise in the doorway draws my attention and I glance over to see Linc coming through the door. He rushes over to Rocky.

"I told you to wait for me." He crouches down next to him. "Where are you hit?" Nash and Jesse step back to give them some space. He lifts Rocky's side up as Rocky groans in pain which makes Callie cry. Her small hand touches his cheek. Linc cusses when he sees the blood. "Where are the paramedics?" he asks the room and then turns back to Rocky. "Daniel, don't you fucking die." Linc looks over at Callie and she starts crying harder. He reaches out to her and caress her hair. "Shush, darlin. It's okay."

"You'll have to protect her now," Rocky says as he looks at Linc. Then he turns to Max. "If they think there's a threat, they'll keep coming for her." His breathing starts to slow and he looks down at Callie and pulls her closer before leaning down and kissing her on top of her head. She climbs up higher and tucks her face in his neck. She whispers something in his ear and he smiles and closes his eyes.

"Promise me, please," he says and turns to Max. "I know what I did. To Jaycee and Abigail. I'll burn in hell for it. I wish I could take it back. I wish I could have had the life you're going to have with her. I still gotta ask though."

My dad steps forward. He's a big old bear but he has four sons. I know he's feeling something for Rocky despite all that happened. Knowing we what know now, that it's not entirely his fault. He leans down.

"What do you need, son?" Rocky stares at my Dad and I see him mouth "son" as a few tears slide out of Rocky's eyes and into his hair. Linc moves in closer and

228

Rocky turns to him.

"Son. Did you hear that?" he says to Linc. "I almost killed both his daughters and he calls me son. Our father, never. My only regret was not killing him," he says.

Linc leans down and says inches from his face. "No little brother, he was mine."

"Son, the paramedics are here. Hang on," Dad says as everyone starts to stand back.

Max starts to pull Callie away put she tightens her grip on Rocky. "Come on baby. We have to take Rocky to the doctor," Max tells her and Callie raises her head and looks at Rocky with tear-stained eyes.

"You have a owie?"

"Just a little one baby," he says, weakly.

I start to cry as Callie leans down and kisses Rocky's cheek and then looks back up at him with hope in her eyes. "Betwer?"

"All better, baby," he says and smiles at her and then looks back at Max. "Promise me." He stops and looks over at me, then Callie and back at Max. "Take care of my girls for me."

"She's my girl, asshole," Max says as Rocky tries to laugh and then moans.

"Yeah, she's your girl." His gaze falls on Callie. "But she's mine." He coughs and some blood falls from his mouth before he says his last words "Take care of my baby sister for me." He pulls Callie closer and then releases her.

Uncle Brock steps forward and picks her up. It's like she knows he's gone because this time she goes with him. I look as he takes Aunt Paige's hand and leaves as the paramedics come in and start working on Rocky.

His baby sister?

CHAPTER TWENTY-TWO

It's late evening and I'm sitting at my dad's house on one of his lawn chairs thinking back to the last year and all that's happened. Abigail is getting ready to move to Lubbock and the family is having a barbeque for her before she flies out in the morning.

It's been three months since that terrifying day at my grandma's when Rocky's saved us. He earned his redemption as far as I'm concerned. I think he earned it from everyone. I know Abigail and I have forgiven him. My mind wanders back to the first time I met him at the dance hall. When my dad came over because my brothers were worried. I remember him saying, "No worries, if I had a sister I'm sure I'd be protective or her, too." Protect her is exactly what he did. Finding out he had a sister was what pulled him out of the dark and back into the light. Callie was his salvation.

After Rocky's shooting, Linc came forward with the information that linked Cole and Callie to Linc and Rocky. Sasha Rowe, Cole and Callie's mom was a nurse who worked with Dr. Jennings and eventually became one of his victims along with Cole. We've learned she loved her children dearly and was an amazing mom. Their great aunt turned over pictures to Aunt Paige and Uncle Brock of her and Callie for safe keeping. One day while looking through the pictures with my Aunt Paige, I froze on one. As I studied it, tears filled my eyes. It was the woman I saw at Cole's funeral. The one that hugged the man holding the tricycle. My heart burns in pain as I realize that was the moment she realized her fate and let go so that her daughter could have something better.

The people that showed up at my Grandma's house that day are gone. I never saw anyone's faces except for the deputy and the man that Rocky killed. The deputy is gone; the police say he's probably hiding out in Mexico. There's a warrant out for his arrest for the attempted murder of Sheriff Cullens. He almost died that day, but after eight hours of surgery repairing damage the hollow point bullet caused, he's back at work and doing well. With Rocky gone, and not going after anyone, it's been quiet. The police have gathered evidence on everyone involved, as well as a list of the people that were used as guinea pigs. Hopefully, they will be able to get them some help. Captain Walters and I have had lunch a few times since everything happened and he keeps me updated on what he can as the investigation continues. This story has been in the local headlines off and on for weeks and even made the national news. Each time the police make another arrest on the case, it'll fire back up in the media for a couple of days. I'll be glad when it's finally over.

I've been back to work at Dan's Grocer for a while and Max did end up reenlisting after talking to my brothers and dad about his concerns about being away from me...leaving me alone. I'm so proud of him and his service.

I'm so glad he decided to stay in.

A couple of weeks after Rocky was taken away by the paramedics, we started moving forward with our wedding plans and the building of our home. The foundation is set, the frame is up and the brick is set. Now we're working on the interior and picking out furniture. It's a beautiful two-story ranch house with white stone walls and blue trim. It's has a covered front porch and Max says as soon as he can, he's hanging a porch swing for me. My dad's company, McGinty Construction, should have it finished and ready for us to move in just in time for the field next to it to be covered in bluebonnets. Just like I always dreamed of having. Our wedding is planned for June of next year.

Last weekend was Bradley and Connor's wedding and the day after tomorrow they're going on a cruise for their honeymoon. They're taking Uncle Brock and Aunt Savannah along with Connor's parents with them as a thank you for always loving and accepting for who they are. Abigail and I had been going with them to cake tasting and such and it was a blast. I think more wedding bells will be ringing for Nick and Abigail soon. Callie is going to be busy being everyone's flower girl.

Callie has flourished and is talking more and more like a little girl. She doesn't seem affected by what happened the day Rocky was taken from her arms but we're watching out for her. Linc has been back a few times and taken her out for ice cream. She now knows he's her brother and they very much adore each other. With Cole and Rocky both gone, Aunt Paige and Uncle Brock agreed they needed each other, needed to know one another. No one in my family ever mentioned to the police about Linc telling Rocky he killed their dad. There were police in the room and if they did hear, they're not saying anything either. I think everyone agrees Dr. Jenning's deserved what he got.

The door opens and Violet walks out holding a small package that she hands to me. I look down and read the front. "Callie McGinty ℅ Jaycee McGinty" and my grandma's address. I raise questioning eyes to her, but she just shrugs her shoulder.

"I went by yesterday but no one was home. When I was pulling out of the driveway, the postman waved so I stopped. He handed me the mail and asked if I would drop it off since there was a package." Violet tells me and then smiles, touching my cheek before turning and going back in the house.

I look down and see no return address but it was mailed from the Texas/Mexico border town of El Paso a few of days ago. I open it as Max walks out of the house and sits down next to me and looks at me in question. "What's that"?

"I don't know. It's for Callie but was sent to my care. The postman gave it to Violet yesterday when she stopped by the house." I say as I open the small box. Inside is a pouch. I pull the string loose and open it, letting the contents fall into my hand. I stare at it for a few moments before reaching down and pulling it up by the chain. Max knows what it is from my description. He sits back in the chair and rubs his hands up and down his face.

"Is that what I fucking think it is?" he asks as I hold it up but don't say anything. "Fuck!"

Yes, I will hold on to this for her, but one day, after you find them all, after she's safe, you can give it to her yourself.

The End

EXTRA CHAPTERS

Sasha Rowe

'I solemnly pledge myself before God and in the presence of this assembly, to pass my life in purity and to practice my profession faithfully. I will abstain from whatever is deleterious and mischievous, and will not take or knowingly administer any harmful drug. I will do all in my power to maintain and elevate the standard of my profession, and will hold in confidence all personal matters committed to my keeping and all family affairs coming to my knowledge in the practice of my calling. With loyalty will I endeavor to aid the physician in his work, and devote myself to the welfare of those committed to my care.'

Five years ago, I stood before my teachers, fellow graduates and my aunt Louise and took "Florence Nightingale Pledge" and it was the best day of my life. I had such big dreams. I was going to save the world.

One year later, I fell in love and that love destroyed my dreams. That love destroyed me and over the last four years, I've watched it destroy life after life. I fell in love with a doctor, a handsome true blue devil. His eyes sparkled like stars. His silver eyes hypnotized me. I fell hard and fast in love with a monster. That monster was Dr. Davis Jennings.

I remember it started as careless flirting, a touch and then a kiss. He shared his dreams of saving the world too. We would talk for hours and share dreams of helping people together. We were going to get married and start a family but I found out too late he already had a family. It devastated me and then his promises started. His lies started. His torture started.

It was his birthday and I had just finished giving him his present. I wore a white lacy bra and panties that day and when I walked into his office and shut the door and locked it, he looked up from his paperwork and smiled. I slipped off the scrubs and walked over to him as he sat back in his chair and pulled me to him. He had just had me, taken me on his desk and I was walking out of his office when a beautiful blonde woman came up with two handsome young men and they were talking amongst themselves. I remember being taken with her smile and I watched her talk to the young men. They were just as smitten with her as she was with them. She was holding a box wrapped in silver wrapping paper with a black bow tied around it. The young men, they looked exactly like Davis. The younger of the two, his eyes, they twinkled silver, like Davis. I knew then. I knew even as I tried to rationalize as to who they were. But I knew. I felt myself die. My heart, it hurt to the point I couldn't breathe. Then she looked up at me and smiled. It took a few moments, but then she knew too.

I watched as her son's closed ranks on her. She swayed and leaned into the oldest of the two young men. No one said a word until Davis opened his office door, startling us.

"Hey, sweetheart." He leaned down and gave her a kiss. "Linc and Rocky," he smiled at them. "What a nice surprise. What are you doing here?"

Still no one spoke. My eyes started to tear but I pulled it together and took a deep breath. This was when I saw a side of Davis I didn't know existed.

"Ms. Rowe, this is Lina, Rocky and Lincoln, my wife and sons. Ms. Rowe is one of our nurses here. She was updating me on a patient and was just leaving." He looked at me dismissively. "Have a nice day, Ms. Rowe." he said as he opened the door and ushered them into his office.

Lina Jennings, his beautiful wife, gave me a sad smile. She was hurt but I think she felt more bad for me. I saw no hate. I think I saw solidarity. Her sons refused to look at me. Both had their hands on their mom's shoulders and arms.

"It was nice to meet you, Ms. Rowe." She extended her hand. When I took hers in mine, my body jolted. It was so warm and soft but her grip was firm. She squeezed my hand. It was a silent gesture between her and I. I remember I held on longer than I should have. She was passing me her strength. I didn't know at that very moment why. Later that day when Davis showed up at my home, I found out.

That day, he came in and when I yelled at him to leave, he hit me. I couldn't believe it. Then it got worse. He told me again and again that if I ever tried to leave him, he'd kill me.

During the next year, the only reason I stayed with him was my Aunt Louise, I owed her after she took me and cared for me after my parents died in a car wreck when I was younger. I loved helping people, caring for people. Giving them hope. I loved my town and I didn't want to leave my home too. I still argued with Davis and I still got hit. One night when I decided to go on living my life, I went out on a date with a paramedic I had met in the hospital cafeteria. When I got home, he beat me so bad I missed work for a week.

After I healed, my aunt talked me into running. I didn't know where I was going. I just drove and the first night I stopped in Baton Rouge and checked into a run down motel. In the middle of the night, I woke to a knock on the door. I froze. It was him and I knew it. He'd found me. I never knew how and never asked because the second he stepped in the room, he slapped me. The beating I took for running was a hundred times worse. The next day, I rode home with him after he arranged for my car to be delivered by a local garage. There were other times I did call the police; but they did nothing to him. Witnesses...always asking for witnesses. It was my word against his. He could have confessed but had enough connections he would never be charged.

I made a choice to wait it out. Surely, he would tire of me. He'd never left his wife so why did he want me. I hoped he'd find another woman, leave me alone. I just wanted to be free and find to true love. I just wanted to be someone's one and only.

Then the day came I received the best and worse news of my life, I was pregnant. I don't know how. I used birth control. Now, later, knowing what I know, he had to have tampered with my pills.

He showed up at my home the day I took the test. He acted so happy. Over the next few months, he became the doting boyfriend and it made me sick to watch. The happy expectant father but refused to allow me to openly say to anyone he was the father. Saying it would hurt his reputation and chances to move up the ladder. He always made promises of "one day." Of course, he never left his wife and sons. Later, he told me Lina Jennings had taken ill and was having problems walking. During my pregnancy, her condition deteriorated to the point she was in a wheelchair. I used that, saying she needed him. I tried to push him away, telling him to go and stay with them, that I'd be fine. I didn't want him. I could never come to terms with being with him anyway. How could I ever live with a man who could hurt me, hurt his wife and sons?

The day my daughter was born was the happiest day of my life. I remember looking at her blonde hair and when her eyes opened, they sparkled silver like her father's, like her brothers. My beautiful, Callie. My beautiful, perfect, Callie. She was the happiest little girl and had the most magnificent laugh. Whenever she giggled, her little button nose would crinkle and out would pop the biggest dimples. She was my life. I took her everywhere with me. People never asked who the father was. I guess in these days and times they made their own assumptions. It didn't matter because we were happy. Whenever Davis came around, I made sure to not upset him. I never wanted her to see him angry. I never wanted to taint her joy. She loved her Daddy too. Sometimes when I would watch them together, I would think that maybe he had a heart but then I would remember and I knew this was all the lie.

The next few months, Davis continued being the doting dad. He came by, spent the night, ate with us and played with her. As she got older, on rare occasion we even took her to the park but stayed off in a secluded area so no one would see us. He brought her gifts and clothes and gave me money. I put the money aside for her. I didn't want it. To me, it was tainted but one day, it might mean something to her.

I sat back and watched the ticking time bomb that was Davis. I trusted not one thing he was doing, but he had yet to show his cards. He told us over and over how much he really wanted us to be a family, but he couldn't leave Lina, not now.

Soon, I became sick too. I didn't know what was going on. I was always healthy and active except for the occasional cold or flu. Davis came around less and less and I had to leave Callie with my Aunt Louise more and more. It broke my heart. My pain was horrible. Aunt Louise begged me to go to the doctor and I did, time after time. All they would give me was pain medication. They told me they couldn't find anything wrong. Suggested a physiatrist; that I having somatic pain or just trying to get pain medication. I knew something was wrong. With both Lina Jennings and myself becoming so terribly ill, I suspected Davis was somehow behind it but I didn't know how. Then I remembered my birth control pills and how he tampered with them. The times he brought me dinner or if I was sick, brought me medication. He did something, I was positive. I had to find a way to prove it.

One fateful afternoon I went looking to get proof on my own. I wanted answers before I said anything, but all the while still praying I was wrong. That my daughter's father was not this evil.

I rode up the service elevator and waited around the corner for an opening. It came sooner than I expected. Davis walked out of his office and called over to a nurse that he had meetings and wouldn't be back for the rest of the day. He disappeared down the hallway and I made my way to his office.

Once in, I rummaged through the papers on his desk and his file cabinet. I had just opened his bottom desk drawer and saw a locked metal box when I heard voices. Davis' voice and two other men. They were coming back to his office. One I recognized but couldn't place, and one that had a slight Spanish accent. I closed the drawer and ran into his private bathroom and hid in the shower stall. The conversation that took place was so shocking that when it was over, I fell against the wall and slid down. So much so that when Davis came in and found me and carried me to the sofa in his office, I didn't react.

That day I found out he and others were nothing

more than drug manufacturers and dealers. He and others were trying to create a new drug but they were not chemists working in a lab. They were testing their drugs for pain with high addictive's on unknowing humans, using trial by error. I was a lab rat, Lina Jennings was a lab rat, his sons were lab rats as well as many, many others. They were experimenting on us. That day, when he found me, he threatened to take Callie from me, he threatened to hurt her and my Aunt Louise if I ever spoke about what I heard; but if I kept my mouth shut, he'd leave Callie, me and my Aunt alone. He took me that day and I couldn't even fight. Six weeks later, I found out I was pregnant again. I ran and hid, but I was too sick to take Callie with me and that shattered my heart.

Nine months later, after living in pain and hiding, only sneaking back into town for quick visits with Callie after random phone calls from throw away phones, I found myself in labor and walking into the hospital's emergency room. After a short labor, my darling son was born but he was very sick. He was taken away for tests and I laid there, legs still in stirrups, looking at the door that my son just left through when Davis walked in. I don't know how he knew I was there but I was learning he had connections everywhere.

"He won't live very long. Leave the hospital now before they start asking questions. If you don't, I'll come for Callie. If you talk, I'll kill her." He walked up to the edge of my bed and grabbed my face in a tight grip. "If you ever talk about anything, I will do to her what I did to you." He pushed my face away. "Go back to your house, get some things and go back into hiding, Sasha." He truly was a man with no soul.

I broke down into sobs. My son won't live? What have I done? I didn't even get to hold him. My God, I didn't even see him. After the nurse came back, I was moved to a room. I was told my son was in very ill in the NICU. As soon as the nurse brought in my belongings, I got up from the bed and slipped back on the maternity clothes I came in just hours ago and walked down to the nursery. There he was, my son.

My beautiful son, hair blonde like his sister, tubes running out of his head and ankle and cords hooked up to his little chest and back. He was sleeping soundly. I watched him for a while and then made my way to the fire exit and took the stairs down to the car garage. I walked out of the hospital with little soul left. I had to stop Davis. I had to fix what he broke. I would have my vengeance and he would never touch Callie.

After hiding away in a cheap hotel for a couple of days and allowing myself to heal some, I walked into the local gun shop and bought a gun. The law wouldn't allow me to buy bullets that day so I would have to wait. Later, I went to a small private doctor's office that accepted cash payments. I couldn't take the pain anymore. I went in and after getting checked and a prescription for pain medication, I went to the pharmacy to fill it. As I sat waiting, I planned. I would wait, give him time to settle, then I was coming for him.

Three nights later, I sat in the motel room watching

the news when I bolted up in bed. My mouth dropped open when I heard what the news reporter said. "Local prominent doctor, Dr. Davis Jennings, was found murdered in his home this morning. Police are saying it appears he knew his attacker as there was no forced entry. Investigations are underway." For the first time in years, I smiled.

I could go back to Callie and my son. I could have my life now. Finally, I felt free.

The next day I went to the hospital to see my son. I was in pain, my body hurting so bad that I could hardly walk but I wanted to hold him.

When I got to the nursery, I stood and looked through the window, tears filling my eyes, my heart warmed and broken at the same time.

There was a beautiful woman, with long dark hair and a stunning face, and she was holding my son, rocking him. Her lips were moving, I couldn't hear what she was saying but I knew, I knew she was praying. She was praying for my son and as she prayed, I prayed with her. I walked out of the hospital, I knew he was better off with her than me. My body was deteriorating. I don't know what Davis gave me but my body was failing. I could feel it; I was dying.

Later that day, I went to see Callie but she was gone. My Aunt Louise was in tears and frantic. She said a man, a Hubert Doss, a judge she'd seen in the newspapers and on TV was looking for me and threatening to hurt Callie if she didn't tell him where I was. In a panic, she called family services to come get Callie. She was hysterical, begging for forgiveness. Saying she was a weak, old woman and couldn't protect her and hadn't a clue to where I was. She didn't know what to do so she thought turning her over, they would protect her until I came back. After calming her down, I went and bought bullets and went back to my motel room.

That night, I realized, even if Davis was dead, others knew Callie was his and that I possibly knew things. She would never be safe. She would always be a weapon one way or another if they knew she was Davis' daughter.

The next afternoon, I decided to to see my son one last time before I followed through with what I knew I had to do. I walked into the hospital and up to the nursery window but my son was gone. In the room, I saw a nurse I went to nursing school with, Jenny. When she saw me, she smiled. She came to join me in the hallway.

Before she could talk I asked in panic, "Where is the baby boy?" I asked, my eyes darting around the nursery. "Is he out for tests? Did he leave?" Her face filled with compassion as she realized who I was asking about; who I was. "Where is he?" I yelled. "Where is my son?"

"Sasha, I'm sorry, honey. He passed away two days ago." Tears spilled down her cheeks.

I dropped to my knees and cried. Davis told me he wouldn't live but that beautiful woman prayed. I prayed. Did God *not* hear us?!

"Sasha, he was so sick, honey. So, so sick." She sank

to the floor next to me. She didn't ask me about drugs, she knew in her heart I would never do that. She knew the real Sasha.

"Where is he, Jenny?" I looked up at her, barely seeing her through my haze of tears.

"Oh, Sasha, the family, they took him. They thought you abandoned him. He didn't even have a name. They named him, begged the judge to let them adopt him even after he passed. You didn't fill out the paperwork, but people recognized you. Looked for you but you vanished. They're having a funeral for him the the day after tomorrow, Sasha. I'm so sorry." She pulled me to my feet and wiped away my tears.

"Who are they, Jenny?" I beg but she doesn't say anything. I watch as her eyes search my face. She knows she's crossing a line if she tells me. Finally, she relents. "The McGinty's. Brock and Paige McGinty adopted him. They named him Cole Jaxson McGinty." My body jerks with a sob. What a beautiful strong name. "They're holding a service for him out at the Church of Christ in Kerr County. Some of us are going. Sasha, I'm so sorry." She pulls me into a hug and holds me until my sobs subside.

I make the drive to Kerr County and stand back in the back of the church that is overflowing with people and stare at my son, forever sleeping in the smallest most beautiful coffin I've ever seen. The altar is filled with toys and the church with blue balloons. I feel my face wet with tears, but I'm cold and numb. The preacher says such beautiful words, yet I feel nothing but deep pain. As

247

everyone starts to file out, I stand staring at my son, wishing with everything I had that I'd gotten to hold him just once. Jenny spots me at the same time I spot her. She starts to walk over, but I give a tight head shake, silently begging her to stay away. She nods, looks down and walks away. I don't want anyone to know who I am or why I'm here. One day, they'll all know.

After the service, I follow the congregation as they make their way to a tiny cemetery. I watch as my son is carefully carried and placed next to his grave. There are so many people here. I stand just outside the metal gates and watch as a man walks up holding a guitar. He pulls the strap over his shoulder and when he starts to strum, everyone goes silent. The song is perfect. My baby son's life was too short and filled with pain. I listen as everyone joins in softly singing the chorus of *Go Rest High On That Mountain*.

I know I shouldn't, but after, I follow the cars to a beautiful plantation style home. Food and gifts are brought in; all for a little girl. Near the porch, my eyes roam over the endless mountain of dolls and clothes. A man walks up with a red tricycle with ribbons hanging from the handlebars and it has a tiny horn and basket on the front. I already know, but it's confirmed when I hear the man say, this is for Callie and hands it to the lady collecting items on the porch. I hope she likes it, he says. All I can think is, she'll love it. I stare at the bike, my vision blurry with tears. He sees me, and he walks over. He pulls me to him in a side hug and then wipes my tears with his thumb.

"Aw, darlin', don't cry. It's just a bike." I wipe away more tears and then pull him into a hug and hold on. I know I startle him but he hugs me back. This total stranger showing me kindness. This is who my Callie will be with.

Before I let him go. I whisper in his ear, "No, it's not just a bike, it's a beautiful bike and it's everything." I let him go and get in my car.

Days later, after doing research to get some information on Judge Hubert Doss, I go back to the doctor for more pain medication and get it filled. I drive to Judge Doss' home and sit outside. He's not home so I wait until I see him pull into the driveway, get out of his car and walk inside. He's actually a handsome man, with salt and pepper hair. He's tall but not thin. How could someone like him be filled with so much be so evil. But none of that matters now. Time is up for both of us. I need to find out who else knows about Callie. I get out of my car and ring the doorbell. When it opens and he sees me he gives a satisfied grin. "I knew you'd come, follow me. We need to talk." he says.

I stay silent as we walk to his office. He sits behind his desk and I sit across from him in one of the two chairs. He's looking down at some papers on his desk as I pull my gun from my purse and aim at him. When he looks up, he laughs, so I shoot him in the shoulder. He jerks back in the chair and cusses and then reaches down and pushes something underneath his desk, a silent alarm I'm guessing, so I shoot again and hit him in the other shoulder while still calmly sitting in my chair. The minute I fired that first shot,

I sealed his fate, and mine. No turning back now. I have to protect Callie.

"You fucking bitch!" he bellows. "The police will be here any second so you better fucking run or be prepared to go to prison. I'm a fucking judge. I run this town. You're going to be sorry," he says while slumped back in his chair. Now I recognize his voice as the one I heard talking to Davis and the man with accent the day I was hiding in the shower in his office. I sit and stare at him as he tries to get up but can't. Minutes later, I hear the sirens so I better get down to business.

"Who else knows Davis was Callie's father?" I ask calmly with the gun still aimed at him.

"Fuck you. I'm not telling you anything," he says trying to sound brave, I put another bullet in him and he screams out in pain.

"Better tell me or else you'll be dead before they even make it in here," I say while leaning back in my seat.

"I don't know," he cries. "Me, just me!" he quickly says when I hold the gun up again.

"You know, I don't believe you," I close my eyes and sigh as I take the bottle of pain pills from my purse and twist off the top. His phone starts ringing and I lean back as he reaches out to answer and groans in pain from the bullet in his shoulder.

After he answers I tell him to put it on speaker. He does what I ask. "Judge Doss, this is the police. Is everything okay?" He starts to answer but stops when I point the gun at him.

"No, he's not okay. I've shot him three times and he's bleeding a lot. I just need him to answer one question and then I'll let him go and you can get him help."

I hear shuffling and then another voice. "Hello, this is Captain Kebodeaux." he says and I hear more shuffling. "Would you like to tell me your name and let me see if I can help you?" he asks cautiously.

"My name is Sasha Rowe and Judge Doss here is working with others in this town manufacturing and distributing drugs. He was working with Dr. Davis Jennings. They've poisoned me while using me as a lab rat and that killed my son. I need to make sure my daughter is safe. I need to know they won't use her as a weapon because of who she is and what I know."

Because I don't know who to trust, I don't tell him Callie is Davis' daughter only that she's important to these evil bastards.

The sound of tires squealing outside signals the arrival of the police. I know what's going on. They've surrounding the house, looking for a way in to save this piece of garbage. I hear Captain Kebodeaux take in a breath and then he shocks me.

"Sasha, I need you to listen to me. We know what's going on in this town. There are investigations underway. We know Judge Doss is dirty. We can help you."

"With all due respect, you could be involved too. I don't know who is friend and who is foe, but I do feel something that's telling me I can trust you, Captain Kebodeaux, and we both know none of them will see the inside of of a jail cell. All I need is one thing; I need to know my daughter will be safe." I sit and wait. I can hear rustling outside. They're getting close.   "Captain Kebodeaux, whatever they did to me is not curable. I'm dying and I still don't have any answers. They also did something to Lina Jennings, her sons and others. As for me, I'm a nurse and I know I don't have long. My pain gets worse every day and I can feel my body failing. I would like you to promise me one thing. I want your word and then I'll end this." Almost a whisper I ask him, "Just promise me one thing, please?" I plead.

His voice is soft, gentle, and full of kindness. He knows what I'm about to do and he's giving it to me. "What would you like, Sasha?"

I raise the bottles of pills to my mouth and start taking them a few at a time. My tears helping me swallow them down. I manage to take all forty pills. No way back. Before the effects sit in, I answer him. "Promise me, Captain Kebodeaux, promise me that you will make sure, Callie, my daughter, goes with the McGinty's. I know they'll love and protect her. Make sure they adopt her as soon as possible. The sooner she carries their name, the safer she'll be. Watch out for her, please. I'm giving you my permission. I'm giving up my rights to her but not my love. Please, promise me. Protect her from these monsters." I take in a shuddering breath as tears pour from my eyes. "This is my deathbed declaration. This is my dying wish."

I wait, I can barely see through my tears, but I know that Judge Doss is trying to move from his chair, but I don't do anything. I wait. Then I hear the words I need to end this.

"You have my word, Sasha. I promise you I will make sure Callie is taken care of. That your wishes are followed." he says softly as he clears emotion from his throat. "I'll protect her. I promise."

With that, I empty every bullet I have into Judge Doss. I watch as he falls from the chair, eyes open, but dead. I hear the door being busted open and I toss the gun to the floor. I slump in my chair; my breathing is shallow. It won't be long because I'm already halfway dead from what they did to me. Maybe I'm weak for not fighting harder but I'm so tired. I just need the pain to stop. I just need Callie to be safe and as long as I'm alive, she won't be.

My body falls from the chair to the floor. Police rush in and head for Judge Doss and all I can think is, too late, he's in hell. My eyes lock onto one of the men as he makes his way to me, gun raised and he's dressed in black. He kicks my gun away and then drop to his knees beside me. I look at him as my breathing becomes even more shallow.

"Ma'am, where are you hurt?" He starts checking me over while talking. "I'm Officer Bradshaw but you can call me Johnny, okay?" He stops checking when he sees something and I watch as he reaches over and picks up the pill bottle and reads it. "Sasha?" I look up at him through the slits in my eyes that have become heavy and are closing. "Sasha, please tell me you didn't take all of these." One hand goes to my throat, feeling for my pulse and with the other he wipes the hair from my face, cupping my cheek tenderly as my eyes slip closed. "Sasha, stay with me. Help is almost here."

I manage to slightly open my eyes and look up at Johnny, but then I sense, more than see, a light and it's warmth surrounds me. A brilliant silhouette comes into my view and he's holding hands with a little boy. The little boy smiles at me, his silver eyes sparkling and he reaches for my hand.

Johnny calls out one more time. "We need help here! Hurry!" I feel his breath on my face as he pleads. "Sasha, please, hang on." he begs as I feel my last bit of air leave me.

In that moment I think back to the preacher's words at Cole's service when he said, 'I'm sure God himself comes for the children.'

I walk to them and take Cole's hand and my pain slips away. I smile down at him as Cole, my son, pulls me into the light.

Daniel and Lincoln

I hear the door open but don't look up. I know it's my brother. I can't look at him. I can't face the disappointment I know I'll see in his eyes. Maybe even hate. They think I'm a monster but I'm not and at the same time I am. I know what I've done to him, my brother, and at one time, my best friend. I tried my best to protect him but then tried to kill him. It didn't matter what happened to me but I failed anyway. I failed them all. Our Mom sits in a wheelchair and he's left me. I betrayed him. I betrayed her. I betrayed them all. I never understood why. How the soul in me grew so dark. My dad told me it was for the greater good. Told me I would be a hero. Now, I know he was only trying to help himself as he turned me into a villain.

"Rocky." Linc says and although he can't see it, I recoil at him using the name. I used to be his Daniel.

I don't move, keep my head down, looking at the papers spread out over the table. He comes over and sits next to me on the sofa. I can see he's trying to be brave but he's scared shitless of what I might do. I don't blame him. He doesn't see Daniel anymore.

"How?" Linc asks while looking down at all the papers.

I'm looking at the papers but I don't need to. I've read each one a hundred times. But he's not asking about the papers.

He wants to know how I'm alive.

Dr. Jennings. Our bastard father is how I'm alive.

"Dad." I say the one simple word and he knows.

The day I was shot by the police and went off the cliff into the lake. The day I almost destroyed a family. The day I almost killed my brother and two women. Abigail, the sister of the one person I ever truly loved, my Jaycee. That day, inside my head, a battle raged. I could hear one side telling me to stop what I was doing. Stop the path I was on and the other side was yelling at me, causing me to feel rage, screaming at me to fight. Hurt them if they tried to take her from me. To take her if she tried to leave me. After I was shot and went off the cliff, I managed to float on my back using what little strength I had and drift down the water along with the current, eventually coming close enough to a small rocky bank to pull half my body out of the water. I could hear them searching for me, their voices, their footsteps. A helicopter was flying over back and forth. I was weak but in my head I was screaming, over here! Come get me! Stop me! Then I turned to the side and saw blood, my blood, sliding down the rocks into the lake. Either way, it won't be long. Whether I die or they find me, it ends.

I woke up to find myself in a cabin. Lying in a bed with an IV hooked in my arm. I remember forgetting for a few minutes and closing my eyes. Thinking I'd been asleep and had a nightmare but then I heard movement and slowly looked over to see I was still in my nightmare and he was standing there, looking down at me, shaking his head. Showing me how pathetic he thinks I am. He's right.

"Over a woman," he says in disgust and sticks his hands in the front trousers pockets. "Thought I taught you better. But it doesn't matter. You're back. You always come back. Couldn't even escape on a ship in the middle of the Pacific Ocean. No matter how long or how far, you'll come back, even death, you can't escape, Rocky. I'll bring you back one way or another. Now, you'll have to work undercover but you'll be okay. You'll just live in the shadows." He pulls his hands from his pockets and sits down on the edge of the bed and reaches over to check the spot where there's a catheter near my hand. Anyone on the outside would think it was a gesture of caring but I know he's just protecting his own investment.

I look away from him. Why couldn't I have died? Even going to hell, because God would never allow me in Heaven, would be better than this.

"Yes, sir," I say. My words barely come out. I need water.

He helps me sit up and I feel stiffness in my shoulder and stomach. I manage to sit up just enough to take a few sips and then lean back against the headboard of the bed. I look around, not sure where I am.

"You're at Judge Doss' cabin about three miles from our place. When I got news of your stunt, I called up some of Andres' men. Had them comb the area looking for you. When you didn't turn up for a few hours, the police gave up the search for the night presuming you were dead, but I knew you weren't. Andres had his men come out and they searched all night along the banks where the current flowed. I knew you'd follow that," he tells me as he stands and walks over to the window and looks out. "You managed to float into an alcove just a few hundred yards from the dam wall. Had yourself tucked away in a nook. They were just about to give up when they heard you praying. Said you were asking God for forgiveness." He looks back at me. "Rocky, God will never forgive you for the things you've done just like he won't forgive me." He makes his way back over to me. "And that's okay." He glances back out the window and then at me. "Got you up here, removed the bullets and stitched you up. Took three...shoulder, arm and side. That police officer was a terrible shot."

"Jaycee," I say her name like it's being torn right from my heart. I can't believe I killed her. I feel my eyes fill with my tears. Jesus, what have I done. I lean my head back and close my eyes. I feel the drops sliding down my face, my body jerking in a sob.

"Boy, calm down. She's alive. Both she and her sister are fine." he says, exasperated as he sits down in the chair next to my bed.

I jerk my head to look at him. "Alive?" I beg him to be telling me the truth.

"Yes, Rocky. They both survived your ridiculous jealous rampage. Jaycee is back home and living with Blue Bradshaw. You need to forget about her. Her sister, Abigail, is back home too. Forget about all of them. Rocky, if Jaycee is going to be a distraction, I'm going to have to take care of that. Don't make her a problem. I don't like problems," he says while staring at me.

And he would. He'd have someone kill her without blinking an eye. He's in deep with the Mexican drug cartel. He has connections all over this state and into Mexico. His threats have kept me doing his will for as long as I can remember. It started with him hurting my mom, then Lincoln. He never expected me to step up being the youngest, but I did. I love my mom and brother so I did what he told me. Sometimes it was as simple as letting him inject me with something or swallowing a pill, making deliveries, checking on shipments or roughing someone up that upset him. I remember those early days. My early teenage years I remember feeling my body burn from the inside as the chemicals made their way through my system. He would take me to a private lab not far from the hospital he worked at. Everyone knew him at this place. There were others beside me. His guinea pigs. He only stopped when a fellow doctor said that I couldn't take anymore or there would be permanent damage to my mind and then there would be questions. As soon as I was of age, I ran off to the first recruiting station and joined the military, but it was too late. The damage had been done and I came back home and accepted my fate. A monster had been created. Inside my mind a constant battle waged. He made me his soldier. His drug runner and enforcer.

Now, weeks after the shooting, weeks after my dad's death, I sit in our family's cabin looking through papers I found hidden under some floorboards beneath the claw tub in the master bathroom. I knew he'd have something somewhere. I tore this place apart and couldn't find them. I had just about given up and was standing in the master bath remembering how much Jaycee loved the tub.

I remembered that first day, the most beautiful day of my fucked up life, thinking how much I couldn't wait to bring her back up after I got done dealing with Kelly. I was going to run her a bath, light candles, and love her. I feel my breathing become heavy. I walked over to the tub and dropped to the floor. I'm not sure how long I sat there but I kept thinking about Jaycee. Finding something. Finding answers. It's like a voice whispered in my ear to look underneath the tub. I felt along the floor and finally came across a loose board. I pushed the tub as back, surprised at how easily it moved. The pipes moved along with it, but just enough so they didn't break. I pulled one board back and then another and reached in and pulled out a fire safe metal box. Without putting the boards back, I lifted the box and carried it into the family room. After picking the lock I lifted out file after file.

Now two days later after sending him a text from a burner phone, I sit here with Linc. He needs to know.

I've been sitting here for hours now going over everything with Linc. When he got to my file simply marked 'Daniel', he lost it. He's been apologizing nonstop. I don't blame him. I don't blame anyone except the monster who did this to me. Our father.

Finally, I hand him the last file.

I watch as it hit him. The veracity of what's in that file. All the puzzle pieces start coming together.

"He was breeding new lab rats," I say in disgust.

"He killed him and he was probably going to kill her, eventually." Linc says in shock.

"They'll come after her." I tell him. "They'll come looking for these files. If they find out about her, they'll use her as leverage. I'm sure someone knows about her."

"They already have. Someone tore the house apart." he says and looks back at me. "And his office." He sits back against the couch. "What are we going to do, Daniel? We have to protect her."

It's a punch to the gut to hear him call me Daniel again and I cough back the emotion. I have nothing to lose now and he has everything. He has to be there for Mom and her.

I can never come out of the shadows so I'll destroy them all from there, the dark.

"Lincoln, we're not going to do anything." I look him dead in the eye. "I am."

I pick the most important paper up and take one last look. Memorizing every single name. They will all pay. I drop the paper back down and stand up.

"I have to protect her." I say while walking over and looking out the back bay window.

"Do you know where she is?" he asks.

"Yes, I know where. Look at the very bottom of the last page."

I watch as he reads it and then as it hits. "What?" he asks in shock and I walk back over and drop down into the chair across from him.

"Both of them." I say and watch as his eyes dart from me to the paperwork to the floor and finally back to me.

"Brock and Paige McGinty adopted our brother and sister." he says.

"Cole passed away but they continued with the adoption, gave him a proper burial. Their mother, Sasha Rowe," I tap the name listed on the file. "Can't be found but I'm pretty sure she's that nurse we met that one day, his birthday. I think he called her, Ms. Rowe. Their mother is Sasha Rowe. It has to be the same person. Do you remember?" He nods. "Now, the McGinty's are fostering Callie. Waiting to get the clear to adopt her officially, but she's already a McGinty." I say trying to gauge his reaction. Will he want to step in and raise her? I hope he leaves her be. If he could see what I saw that afternoon.

Relief sweeps through my body when he finally speaks. "They'll love her. Protect her. Give her the kind of family a child deserves. The kind of childhood we never had."

Nothing could prepare me for what he says. Never, would I have been prepared for his words. Disbelief and despair follow.

"Daniel, there are some things you need to know," he says with worry. "We both know why now, but things are still what they are and you need to know everything that went down after that day."

I thought I knew the level of destruction I caused to everyone but what little bit of humanity I had left in body evaporates and is filled with vengeance and hate when he tells me the one thing that destroys all that's left.

"Daniel, when Jaycee was recovering in the hospital, after you left her in the field, she found out something. I only know because I overheard Abigail tell Nick one afternoon when I was allowed to get out of bed and walk around. I walked down to her room to see how she was, when I overheard the three of them talking." He drops his head for a few seconds before looking up and wiping his hand down his face. "Jaycee was pregnant, with your baby but lost it when..." he looks away from me without finishing.

I stand and stare at him and then let out a roar that is so thunderous I'm surprised the walls don't crumble and drop to my knees. I fucking killed my own baby. Jesus fucking Christ! I killed my own baby? For a few seconds my wall comes completely down and I find myself sobbing. Sobbing for my mom, Lincoln, my baby and Jaycee. Eventually I wipe my face, stand and walk over and grab my riding jacket and gloves from the table.

"Daniel, what are you doing?" he asks while slowly standing. "You need to stay away from Jaycee. I'm sorry but she's happy, really happy. Leave her be."

I know he's right and it fucking kills me to know I can never have her. She hates me. I hate me and I will never be able to come out of the shadows. I owe her happiness and it breaks me even more to know that it's going to be with another man. I saw it for myself.

I couldn't help it. I knew it was stupid when I walked into that restaurant. I just wanted one look at them, the woman I loved and the little girl I had just found out was my little sister. I had followed her grandma from their house to this place. I stood back in the shadows which have become my domain, watching as all her family arrived and went in. No one noticed me. Why would they? My hair is now down past my shoulders and I have a full beard. I look nothing like the clean cut son of a doctor I was just a few months ago. Now, when people see me, they walk the other way, scared. My outside finally matches my inside. Dangerous. Yes, walk the other way.

I made my way in and stood at the bar watching Callie with the McGinty's. She was beautiful in boots with a big bow in her hair. Her eyes, her eyes they were just like mine. I know I had to be smiling as I watched her wrap every single one of the McGinty men around her little finger. I watched one of the guys, the one with Abigail whisper something in Callie's ear and then she giggled. He walked over like he was going to kiss Abigail on the cheek but then gave her a raspberry. Callie started laughing as Abigail wiped her cheek and slapped the guy's arm. Then Abigail picked Callie up and pretended not to know she was about to do the same thing. When she did, she faked surprise and started laughing when Callie giggle and clapped her hands. I felt my chest get tight at the sight and sadden. He taught her something a big brother would teach her and I'm her brother but I'll never share those things with her. I try to convince myself to be happy for her, for all of them. I remind myself who I really am, a monster.

Then Jaycee walked in the room, looking beautiful and glowing. She was so happy. I smiled and my vision went blurry when she held up her hand and everyone started cheering. My baby, my Jaycee deserves this after what I did to her. My girl, and my sister, they both looked so happy. I stood watching for minutes or hours, I don't know how long. I watched as she disappeared down the hallway with her sister and he was behind her. When he came out wearing the most fuckedup shirt, I didn't laugh, I clenched my fists because I wanted to be wearing that dumb shirt. Her brothers were laughing and giving him a hard time and I wanted that to be me. A couple of seconds later Jaycee came out wearing a similar shirt only looking beautiful and Callie came over to them and he picked her up. They looked so happy. I was so caught up just staring that I forgot who and where I was till the glass dropped from her hand and shattered on the floor and I looked to see her staring at me. When Blue pulled from the glass, I made my way out, never looking back.

"I'm not going to Jaycee," I say as I start walking to the back door where my bike is parked.

"Then what are you doing?" he starts walking over to me "Daniel, I just got you back." and he steps up to me and puts his hand on my shoulder, "I don't want to lose you again. We can go to the police. We can get doctors to testify how you were drugged. Get you help. It wasn't your fault."

I see him swallow and his eyes tear. He doesn't understand. The war is still waging in my mind. Just because I'm not raging at the moment, doesn't mean I won't or if I'll be able to control it when it happens.

"Lincoln, look at that list again. It has police, judges, doctors and politicians on it. I would never get a fair trial. I would never trust a doctor or nurse again," I take a deep breath "I need to go." and I step back and watch his hand fall.

"Daniel, what are you going to do? Where are you going to go?" he asks.

"Take all those papers and give them to the cop who shot me. As of right now, he's the only one I trust." I reach down and open the door and step out into the night and make my way to my bike and straddle it.

"And you?" he says stepping out with me but staying on the deck and looking down at me.

"I have some things I got to take care of.," I say as I turn my bike key "then I'm leaving."

"Daniel, what things? Where will you go?" I see

him tense up as he starts down the steps.

I start the bike right as he gets to me. I look over at him with determination and revenge in my eyes.

"I'm going to rain hell down on this town." I say as I look at him. "They're going to pay and I'm going to make sure our sister stays safe, I look away from him when I say. "Lincoln, I won't be back. Don't wait. Don't wonder. Love Mom and Callie enough for both of us."

I turn back and give my brother one last look.

He gives me a tight nod of his head. He knows if Callie is going to stay safe I'm her only hope. It strange to feel like I'm someone's hope but I am.

If you are concerned that someone you care about is experiencing abuse,

please contact your local police department or call:

1-800-799-7233 | 1-800-787-3224 (TTY)

The National Domestic Violence
HOTLINE

ACKNOWLEDGEMENTS

Dennis—My prince, without your support, love and encouragement this dream would never had happened. I love you.

Patrick, Regan and Julia —you are the most amazing thing that ever happened to me. I love you so very much.

Jacob, Wesley, Marci Rae—I do this for you. Grandma loves you.

My family—Thank you so much for your belief in me.

San Antonio, Texas friends and family—I love you all. Thank you for your friendship, love and over-the-top support.

My Virginia family—To my Fort Belvoir family, I love you so very much. Thank you for buying my book and all your encouragement.

Cassia Brightmore—You're awesome. Without your guidance and support this would not have happened. You're brilliant, beautiful and have the best heart. Xo

Judi Perkins—I'm not sure what to say because your gift leaves me speechless. You're amazing.

Lila Rose—I'm so grateful for your guidance and mentoring. You sent me in the right direction time after time. I cannot express how much the gift of your time and advice means to me. I'm so grateful.

Debbie, Kim and Lisa—Ladies, you are awesome! Without your encouragement I would not be here.

To my amazing Fort Belvoir Exchange Family— There was not a single person or a single time that I did not find love and encouragement from you. You were proud of me (I'm crying) and each time you told me so I was on the verge of crying happy tears. I've worked a few places in my life but never have I ever experienced the support and friendships like I have here. Not only by my department, but HR, management, other departments.

Thank you

To the author community for your inspiration—

River Savage, Gillian Jones, Nicole James, Maria Skye, KC Lynn, L.S. Goulet, James H. Waggoner, Mark Greaney, Alex Shaw and so many others.

www.ingramcontent.com/pod-product-compliance
Lightning Source LLC
Chambersburg PA
CBHW021952170626
46808CB00001B/119

* 9 7 8 0 9 9 8 2 5 1 0 1 1 *